HOW TO WIN
THE DATING WAR

BY
AIMEE CARSON

First published in Great Britain 2011
by Mills & Boon, an imprint of Harlequin (UK) Limited,
Eton House, 18-24 Paradise Road, Richmond, Surrey TW9 1SR

© Aimee Carson 2011

ISBN: 978 0 263 88505 7

01-1211

Harlequin (UK) policy is to use papers that are natural, renewable and recyclable products and made from wood grown in sustainable forests. The logging and manufacturing processes conform to the legal environmental regulations of the country of origin.

Printed and bound in Spain
by Blackprint CPI, Barcelona

HOW TO WIN THE DATING WAR
is Aimee Carson's first book
for Mills & Boon®.
Look out for more great titles, coming up soon!

Did you know this is also available as an eBook?
Visit www.millsandboon.co.uk

To my editor, Flo Nicoll.
Thanks for all your hard work and dedication.
And to Dan. Without you none of this would be possible.

CHAPTER ONE

MANEUVERING tools while lying on his back wasn't easy with the relentless stabbing in his chest, and when the wrench slipped, Cutter's hand plowed into the drive shaft. Pain smashed, and the underside of his '71 Barracuda was lit with stars.

"Damn." The muttered word was lost in the rock music wailing in his garage.

Blood dripped from his knuckles onto his T-shirt. He shifted to the right, and his ribs screamed in protest, eliciting a groan of agony as he pulled a rag from the pocket of his jeans, wrapping it around his hand. His chest still sent crippling signals, but—on the good side—the sting in his fingers now took precedence over the two-month-old, lingering ache in his left arm.

Because Cutter Thompson, former number-one driver in the American Stock Car Auto Racing circuit, never did anything half-assed. Even screwing up. He'd ended his career in style, flipping his car and sliding across the finish line on his roof before crashing into a wall.

Pain he was used to. And even if crawling beneath the belly of the 'Cuda went against the doctor's orders, Cutter was going to complete this project even if it killed him.

The music cut off, Bruce Springsteen's voice dying mid-verse, and a pair of high-heeled sandals tapped their way across the concrete toward the 'Cuda. Cinnamon-colored toenails. Nice ankles. Slender, shapely calves. Too bad the rest was blocked by the bottom of the car. The fine-looking legs were most likely encased in a skirt. From this angle, if he rolled his creeper forward, he'd get an eyeful.

And you could tell a lot about a woman by the underwear she wore.

With a delicate squat, knees together, the owner of the legs leaned low until her face appeared beneath the car. Dark, exotic eyes. Glossy, chestnut-colored hair.

"Hello, Mr. Thompson." Her voice was smooth. Warm. Like heated honey. Her smile genuinely bright. The kind of enthusiasm that should be illegal. "Welcome back to Miami."

Welcome home, Thompson. Like a career-ending injury at thirty was a blessing.

Cutter stared at the lady. "You interrupted Springsteen."

Her smile didn't budge. "I'm Jessica Wilson." She paused. "Did you get my messages?"

Jessica Wilson. The crazy lady who wouldn't take no for an answer. "All five of them," he said dryly. He turned his attention back to his work, his tone dismissive, his words designed to send her away for good. "I'm not interested in a publicity stunt," he said firmly. He wasn't interested in publicity, period.

He used to like it. Hell, he'd *lived* for it. And his fans had been fiercely loyal, following him around the circuit and supporting him unconditionally. Sticking with him through thick and thin. The kinds of things parents usually did.

Except for his.

And now what was he supposed to say to the press? Awesome wreck, huh? And how about that stellar suspension the officials had slapped on him? 'Course, that was before anyone knew his split-second decision had cost him more than separated ribs, a fractured arm and a humdinger of a concussion. It had cost him a career.

Pain of a different sort pierced the base of his skull, and regret hollowed out his stomach. Cutter gripped the wrench, awkwardly wrestling with the bolt again. He'd had to go and ruin his dominant hand, too.

Slowly he became aware the lady was still here, as if waiting for him to change his mind. Some people were too persistent for their own good. He tried again. "I'm busy."

"How long have you been working on the car?"

He frowned, thrown by the change in topic. "Fourteen years."

"So fifteen more minutes of a delay won't be too inconvenient?"

Amused, he rolled his head to stare at her. He was trying to be rude and get rid of Little Ms. Sunshine. Why was she still being so friendly? Her eyes were wide. Luminous. The color of melted chocolate. Cutter lowered the wrench warily. "Inconvenient enough."

"As I explained in my messages, the Brice Foundation wants you for their annual charity auction," she went on, obviously undaunted by his attitude. "We need a fifth celebrity to round out our list."

"Five celebrities gullible enough to participate will be hard to find."

She ignored his comment and went on. "I think your participation would generate a lot of excitement, especially as a native Miamian and a national hero."

Cutter's gut clenched. "You've got the wrong guy."

No heroes here. Not anymore. That had ended with his self-destructing, split-second decision on the track. But if she was looking for a night of sex, the fulfillment of a few fantasies, then he was the man for her. Doubtful she was. And right now he wasn't interested in involvement of *any* kind, in bed or out. "My answer is still no."

She stared at him with those big, Bambi, don't-shoot-me eyes. It had to be an uncomfortable position, balancing on the balls of her feet with her chest against her thighs, her head hanging low enough to look under the bottom of the car. But her voice remained patient. "Will you please just hear me out?"

Damn, she wasn't going to go away.

With a frustrated groan, Cutter rubbed a hand down his face. He needed peace. He needed The Boss blaring on the stereo, drowning out the turmoil in his head. And he needed to get the 'Cuda up and running. But he wouldn't get any closer to accomplishing these if the lady didn't leave. Though, much longer in that position and she'd pass out from a lack of blood flow to her brain. At least then he could haul her out of his garage.

But no matter how much he wanted her to go away, he couldn't let a person continue to hold this discussion while impersonating a contortionist. Even if his chest hadn't recovered from the effort it had taken to climb beneath the car in the first place, even if moving would bring more pain, he had to convince her to leave from a standing position.

With a forced sigh and a grunt of agony, he gripped the chassis of the 'Cuda and pulled the creeper on out from beneath the car, wheels squeaking as he went. He rolled off, his ribs screeching louder in protest, and he sucked in a breath… and got hit with her delicate scent. Sweet, yet sensual, infused with a hint of spice. A lot like her voice.

When he finally managed to straighten up, he got a view of her willowy body wrapped in a cool sundress the color of the sky in springtime. Silk clung to her hips and thighs.

Her shoulder-length dark hair framed a delicate face that housed beautiful brown eyes. Classy. Feminine. A girly girl through and through. The visual was almost worth the excruciating pain that now pounded his ribs.

Almost.

She sent him another smile and nodded toward his car.

"Fourteen years is a long time. It looks like it still needs a lot of work."

Cutter's eyebrows pulled together. Sweet or not, no one was allowed to dis his 'Cuda. "Engine's almost fixed." Mostly because when the doctor had delivered the bad news, Cutter had dragged the vehicle out of storage and given himself until the end of the month to get it done. Better than dwelling on his messed-up life. "Be ready for a test run any day now."

She peered in the window. "But there's only a backseat."

"I kissed my first girlfriend there. Happens to be my favorite spot. Just a few more technicalities to take care of."

"Hmmm," she murmured. Stepping back, she glanced at the concrete blocks the car was perched on. "Are tires considered a technicality, too?"

He quirked an eyebrow, amused by her dry tone. "I'll get to it. I've been busy." Busy racing. Ruining a career.

A scowl threatened. Couldn't a man retreat to his garage for a little one-on-one time with his car without a cheerful, pushy woman tracking him down? Maybe if he looked busy she'd go away now.

He rounded the car to where the hood was propped open and twisted off the oil cap. With the clap of heels, she appeared beside him. Ignoring her proximity, and after pulling out the dipstick, he used the rag wrapped around his mashed knuckles to check the level.

She peered around his right shoulder. "Plenty of oil," she said, sounding amused. "Though I doubt you'd lose much since the car doesn't run."

Busted. Not *too* girly a girly girl. "Can't be too careful."

"Words to live by, Mr. Thompson."

"Precisely." Though not exactly his motto until recently. With a self-chastising grunt, he shoved the oil stick back with more force than necessary. "No publicity stunts for me."

"It's for a good cause."

"Always is."

"You haven't even heard the details."

"Don't need to." Refusing to look at her, he screwed the oil cap on. "I'm not doing it."

She placed her hands on the car frame and leaned close, her evocative scent enveloping him. "The Brice Foundation does the kind of work you and your sponsors have always supported in the past. I know if you hear the details, you'll agree."

The optimistic little lady sounded so sure of herself. Cutter straightened and placed his hands on the frame beside hers, finally meeting her face-to-face. Her olive skin tone suggested a distant Mediterranean ancestor somewhere. Even features. High cheekbones. Full mouth, but not too lush. Nice. "I don't have sponsors anymore." He raised an eyebrow to bring his point home. "And you don't know anything about me."

"You started in the ASCAR truck series at seventeen. Two years later you were dubbed someone to watch by *Top Speed* magazine." Her wide, deep-brown eyes held his. "You burst into the stock car series and blazed your way to the top. You're known for your cutting words and for being fearless on the track, earning you the nickname the Wildcard. You've held the number-one rank for the past six years—" a brief hesitation before she went on "—until your accident two months ago when you intentionally bumped your biggest rival, Chester Coon."

Acid churning in his gut, Cutter suppressed the urge to look away. He'd pay for that moment for the rest of his life. He relived it every night in his sleep. The roaring engines. The smell of rubber. And then he spies Chester to his left. Cutter grips his steering wheel...and then he wakes with a jerk, drenched in sweat, heart pounding.

And feeling every one of his injuries as if they were fresh.

But the actual moment of bumping Chester—and fortunately, the crash itself—were a blank. Retrograde amnesia the doctor had called it. A gift bestowed upon him by his concussion.

Or perhaps it was a curse.

His fingers clenched the car frame harder. "The officials should have suspended Chester for the Charlotte incident last year. Damn rookie put everyone at risk when he drove. And then he nearly got another driver killed."

"There was a lot of hard driving the day of your wreck. Everyone knew Chester had it coming."

Surprised, he cocked his head. Jessica Wilson clearly knew the unwritten rules of the track. A familiar niggle of doubt resurfaced. "You're not one of those fanatics who likes to stalk their favorite driver, are you?" After her five messages that was exactly what he'd assumed, though she didn't seem crazy in person. But it could be she was crazy *and* smart enough to hide it. He'd met a few of those along the way. "If so, your charity ruse is imaginative. Though it's hard to beat the fan who snuck past security at the track, picked the lock on my RV and climbed into my bed naked."

The spirited sparkle in her eyes was captivating. "I hope you tossed him out."

Despite his mood, a rusty bark of a chuckle escaped his throat, knifing his still-smarting ribs. He was beginning to like the pushy little do-gooder, overly optimistic or not. "I tossed *her* out." He leaned close, his senses swimming in her scent. "I would have definitely thought twice about getting rid of you."

"I'm a fan, Mr. Thompson," she said evenly. "Not a fanatic." She hiked a brow, loaded with meaning. "And I'm not a groupie."

He dropped his eyes to her mouth. "Too bad. I'd love to have you wrap yourself in nothing but a bow and mail yourself to me in a crate."

She looked at him suspiciously. "You're making that one up."

"Nope." He tipped his head. "The story has been passed around the track for years. Could be just an urban legend though."

She leaned closer, narrowing her eyes, and his unfamiliar urge to grin was strong. Her voice dropped an octave. "And you are legendary for supporting organizations that work with disadvantaged kids."

The do-gooder was back. "And here I thought you leaned closer just to flirt with me."

Her bottomless brown eyes were unwavering. "I never use flirting as a tool."

"Too bad." But he liked her close, so he stayed put. "And I told you, no way will I—"

"These kids need support from role models like you."

Role models.

The words slammed with all the force of his career-ending crash, killing his urge to grin. Outside of setting a spectacular example of how to destroy the single good thing in your life, what did he have to offer the public now? His one claim to fame was gone. He was just a washed-up driver who'd taken a risky move and gone down in a blaze of shame.

Other than an amused glint in his sea-green eyes, Jessica had yet to see Cutter smile. She watched the glint of humor die as the masculine planes of his face hardened.

"Look, lady." Cutter ruffled an impatient hand over closely cropped, light-brown hair. "You have me confused with someone who cares. My sponsors paid me millions. They told me which charities to support. The only person I support is me."

Jessica's smile faded at the egocentric words.

Cutter turned and walked past shelves of car parts and tools, heading in the direction of a utility sink in the corner. "And right now I have a car to fix," he added with a tone of finality.

Disenchantment settled deep in Jessica's chest. So he didn't care. So he'd only thought of his bank account. And maybe his moving words of support in the past were speeches written by a paid writer. This wasn't about her disappointment that an idol of hers wasn't the hero she'd thought. This was about the Brice Foundation Steve had started. And she'd promised him she'd get Cutter Thompson on board. Because she owed Steve.

How many ex-husbands helped their former wife get a business up and running?

Her online dating service had given her a sense of purpose at a time when her life was falling apart. And finding The One for others, in some small way, compensated for her personal failure.

And though she'd vowed long ago that melancholy wasn't allowed, the garage smelled of gasoline and motor oil, stirring poignant memories. Toward the last months of their marriage, Steve had withdrawn, spending more and more time tinkering with his boat. Maybe twenty was a little young for marriage, but Jessica had been confident they could work through anything. She'd been wrong. And Steve had begun to insist he couldn't give her what she needed.

In the end, Jessica had agreed.

But, between her father and her ex, she was used to men and their masculine domains. And Cutter Thompson was man in its rawest form. Long, powerful legs encased in worn jeans. Well-muscled arms. The wide expanse of back beneath his gray T-shirt was a veritable billboard sign for male power. He was a media favorite for his rugged charm, so the blunt honesty wasn't new. But the slight hunch as he walked certainly was. Why was his gait uneven?

Curiosity trounced her good sense. "If it was your arm you fractured in the crash, why are you limping?"

"I'm not. I'm splinting. The torn cartilage between my ribs still hurts like a mother."

At the sink, he turned on the tap, and—without a hiss or a grimace—stuck the mashed knuckles of his right hand under the water. His left arm reached for the soap, and he dropped it twice before a stab of sympathy hit her.

Selfish or not, no one deserved permanent nerve damage from a broken arm.

"Let me," she said as she moved beside him.

His eyes lit with faint humor. "Promise you'll be gentle?"

Ignoring him, Jessica picked up the soap and reached for his bleeding hand. It was large, calloused, and a disturbing sensation curled in her stomach, permeating lower. Neither of them spoke, increasing the crackle of tension. The sound of running water cut the silence as her fingers gingerly cleaned the wounds, finally finishing her task.

The glint in his eyes was bright. "Sure you didn't miss a spot?"

"Quite sure." She calmly dried his hand with a paper towel. "The weakness in your left hand is worse than your publicist let on." Once finished, she looked up at him. "I can see why you decided to retire."

The glint died as an unidentifiable flicker of emotion crossed his expression, but his gaze remained steady, his tone droll. "A man can't drive two hundred miles per hour packed bumper to bumper with an unreliable grip. Keeping a firm grasp on the steering wheel is important."

She looked for some sign of sadness, but there was none. "I'm sorry."

"Happens." He shrugged, a nonchalant look on his face. "I can't complain. I made enough money that I never need to work again."

They stared at each other for three breaths, Jessica fighting the urge to beat a hasty retreat. He'd made his millions. Racing had served its purpose. She knew he was planning to reject her request again, but Steve was counting on her. Despite Cutter's casual air, instinct told her to let the reminder of his injuries—the loss of his money-making career—fade before bringing out her best shot at persuasion…her pièce de résistance.

Her mind scrambled for something to say, and her gaze dropped to the marks on his shirt. "You should wash out the blood before it stains."

"Because it clashes with the motor oil?"

Boy, he had a comeback for everything. "No," she said dryly. "Because blood stains are so last season."

The light in his eyes returned with a vengeance. "Blood is always in style," he said. "And rising from a horizontal position about did me in. I'm just now able to breathe again without wanting to die. If I attempt to pull this shirt over my head, I'll pass out from the pain." He finally flashed the rarely dispensed yet utterly wicked suggestion of a smile. The one that sent his female fans into a frenzy. "So how about you pull it off for me?"

She lifted her eyes heavenward before meeting his gaze. "Mr. Thompson, I spent half my childhood following my father around his manufacturing plant full of men. I'm not susceptible to your brand of testosterone."

And one dream-crushing divorce later, she considered herself fully vaccinated, immune and impenetrable to anyone who couldn't totally commit. She needed someone who was willing to work hard to keep the romance alive.

Egocentric bad boys, no matter how gorgeously virile, had never made it to her list of acceptable dates. While all her friends were swooning over the rebel-de-jour, Jessica had remained untouched. Even as a teen, she'd avoided risky relationships that were destined for failure. She supposed she had her parents' divorce to thank for that.

But she refused to slosh about in dismal misery. Making a plan—being proactive—was the only way to avoid the mistakes of the past. Both her parents'…and her own.

"I don't know, my brand of testosterone is pretty potent,"

Cutter said. "And seduction could go a long way in convincing me to participate."

"Believe me." Her smile was tight. "I have no intention of seducing you."

Cutter almost managed a grin again. "After six painful career accidents, this is the first time I've ever felt like crying."

"Don't shed any tears on my account, Mr. Thompson." Rallying her courage, she crossed to her oversize purse by the stereo, pulled out a folder, and returned to Cutter. She would not be sidetracked. "I'm just here to recruit you." Jessica extracted a photo of an eight-year-old boy with a sweet smile. Without preamble, she continued. "Terrell's father died of cancer. He attends the Big Brothers' program the Brice Foundation supports."

The almost-smile died on his face, and the pause stretched as a wary look crept up his face. "And what does that have to do with me?"

"It's easier to say no to a nameless, faceless child. And I want you to know who you'll be letting down when you refuse to participate." She pulled out a second photo of a freckle-faced kid. One way or another, she was going to get him to agree to the charity event. "Mark is an eleven-year-old foster child attending a program that helps young people learn to find their place in a new home." She paused theatrically, hoping to draw attention to her next statement. "Older kids are harder to place."

"Orphans." Cutter frowned. "You're bringing out bloody *orphans*?"

His response left her feeling hopeful, so Jessica pulled out a third photo—a scowling teen. Dark hair reached his shoulders. Baggy pants hung low on his hips, red boxers visible above the waistband. The belligerent look in his eyes was sharp. If sweet smiles and freckled faces weren't enough, an adolescent with a defensive attitude would be harder to refuse. Not a smidgen of Cutter's history had been overlooked in her quest to get him to agree.

She was on a mission, and Jessica Wilson was famous for following through.

"Emmanuel dropped out of high school," Jessica said. "The Brice Foundation hooked him up with a mentor who took him to see you race." She made sure her face went soft, her eyes wide.

Cutter's frown grew bigger. "Are you trying to work up some tears?"

She blinked hard, hoping she could. "He was getting into trouble street racing." When the tears wouldn't come, she opted to drop her voice a notch. "Just like you."

His frown turned into an outright scowl. "Damn, you're good. And you did your research, too. But the mushy voice is a bit much. I'd respond better to seduction."

Jessica ignored him and went on. "Now he's attending night school to get his diploma." When his face didn't budge, she dropped her pièce de résistance. "He's decided he wants to be a race-car driver…just like you."

Cutter heaved a scornful sigh, and the exaggerated breath brought a wince to his face. He propped a hand on his hip, as if seeking a more comfortable position. "If it will get you to leave so my ribs can commune with an ice pack and some ibuprofen, you can put me down on the list of gullible five."

Mission accomplished. With a flash of relief, Jessica sent him a brilliant smile. "Thank you," she said. "I'll get the packet of information so we can go over—"

"Sunshine." He winced again, shifting his hand higher on his hip, clearly in pain. "We'll have to put off the rest of this discussion until tomorrow. But don't worry…" A hint of amusement returned to his eyes. "I'll leave the offer to remove my shirt on the table, just for you."

CHAPTER TWO

"Hell no," Cutter said.

"But we've already released the press announcement," Jessica said.

The rising sense of panic expanded as she watched Cutter cross his modern living room. And though the room was adorned with leather furniture, glass-and-chrome accents, it was the plate-glass window overlooking a palm-tree-lined Biscayne Bay that took masculine posh to outright lavish.

If he backed out now, it would be a publicity nightmare. "It was announced on the local six o'clock news last night," Jessica went on.

She'd been full of hope when she'd arrived back at his home this evening to discuss the fundraiser. Cutter was clearly feeling better than he had yesterday, no longer splinting as he walked. All she'd had to do was explain the plans for the fundraiser, get him signed on to the social-networking site hosting the event, and then her duty to Steve would be complete. Which meant her dealings with Cutter Thompson would be through.

Wouldn't that have been nice?

Cutter turned to face her, the waterway and its line of luxury-boat-filled docks beyond the window. "You should have waited to announce my participation until *after* you explained how this little publicity stunt was set up."

"We're short on time. We start next week. And I don't understand your problem with it."

His face was set. "I thought it would be the same auction they do every year. Men show up and strut their stuff. Women bid. The Brice Foundation makes money for homeless children, and I get to sit at the benefit dinner with the victorious socialite who doesn't have a clue—or cares—what poor kid her outrageous bid is helping." He crossed his arms, stretching the shirt against hard muscles. "I had no idea I'd have to *interact* with the women competing to win a date with me."

"But that's the beauty of the setup." Jessica rose from the leather couch, unable to restrain the smile of enthusiasm despite his misgivings. She'd worked long and hard to create something that wasn't the usual superficial masculine beauty show. "It's not as demeaning as auctioning off a celebrity like a slab of high-priced meat."

He sent her a level look. "I find nothing degrading about women trying to outbid each other all in the name of scoring a dinner with me."

Her smile faded a bit. "Maybe *you* don't. But I wanted something a little more meaningful. Watching intelligent men prance across a stage in an effort to increase the bidding is an undignified way to raise money."

"You forgot my favorite part: the screaming women." Cutter sent her the first hint of a grin for the evening. "You have to know how to work the crowd. Bring them to the edge of their seats. The key to raking in the dough is to wait until just the right moment to take off your shirt."

His chest was impressive covered in fabric; no doubt he'd made millions for various fundraisers over the years.

Jessica focused on the task at hand. "The board wanted something fresh and new, not the same old thing they've done the past ten years." She crossed thick carpet to stand beside him. "Except for your attendance at the benefit dinner, all the interaction is done online. You engage in a little flirty debate with the ladies competing for you. It's supposed to be an entertaining battle of the sexes over what comprises the perfect date." Her smile grew. That was her favorite part. Since her marital misstep, the study of relationships had become a passion. "For a nominal fee, the public can cast their vote for the 'most compatible.' So the people decide your companion to the benefit dinner, not the socialite with the most money to bid."

It had taken her weeks of brainstorming to finally land on a plan she was proud of, and she waited for some sign of his approval.

"So the masses decide which contestant—a lady I've never met nor will ever see again—I'm most 'compatible' with?" It was obvious from the air quotes with his fingers that he found her plan ridiculous. "Who the hell came up with this Trolling for a Celebrity idea?"

Jessica frowned. "It was my suggestion. And it's supposed to be all in fun, so I'd prefer you use the term *flirting* to *trolling*."

"What the hell do you think flirting is?"

"It's engaging in meaningful dialogue that shows you find a person interesting."

He stared at her. "Maybe if you're twelve. For adults, it's all about sex."

She barely kept the criticism from her voice. "No it's not." She bit the inside of her lip, and inhaled, forcing herself to go on calmly. "There is plenty of data to support the notion that successful people are those who market themselves in a positive manner. Building strong relationships is the key to success, no matter what your goal, be it business, friendship or love. And *flirting,*" she continued with emphasis, "establishing that rapport between two people, proves that the most important aspect of a romantic relationship is effective communication."

Cutter's brows had climbed so high Jessica thought his

eyelids would stretch clear over his forehead. "Who has been feeding you all this bullshit?"

"It isn't bullshit."

"Sunshine, you are up to your black, sooty little eyelashes in it." The amused look in his eyes almost constituted a smile. "You are so Pollyanna-ish you could light the world with the sunbeams that glow from beneath your skirt." His voice turned matter-of-fact. "The attraction between a man and a woman is built on spark, pure and simple. And you can't *communicate* your way around the lack of it."

She'd had plenty of experience with a man who lacked the ability to engage in earnest dialogue. The spark starved without it, and though she'd done everything in her power to prevent the death of her marriage, a small part of her—the part that had *failed*—could never be made right.

Gloom weighed down her heart, and she folded her arms across her chest to ease the load.

Think positive, Jessica. We learn from our mistakes and move on. Don't let Mr. Cynical bring you down.

"Sparks are sustained by emotional and intellectual attraction," she said. "And both are much more important than the physical one."

His eyebrows pulled together in doubt. "What's that have to do with an online flirting fiesta between virtual strangers?"

Jessica inhaled slowly and quietly blew out a breath, regaining control. She'd gotten off track. Convincing him of her views wasn't important. All she needed was for him to follow through on his initial agreement. If he backed out now, the fundraiser would fail before it even started. Hundreds of fans would be disappointed. And then Steve would kill her, because signing Cutter on had been her idea. Steve had thought the retired driver was a risky proposition, but Jessica had always been impressed with Cutter's magnetic, if a little unconventional, charm on TV.

Apparently he was really good at faking it when money was involved.

Lovely to be finding that out *now*.

"Forget that I think the basic concept is flawed," Cutter said, interrupting her thoughts. "We still have several problems. First, I don't know a thing about social networking."

Feeling encouraged, she said, "I can teach you."

"Second, I don't have time for all this online interaction stuff."

"You can do it anywhere, even while standing in line at the grocery store. It takes five seconds to text a question to the contestants. Maybe ten to respond to their answer."

"I don't text."

Stunned, Jessica stared at him. "How does anyone inhabiting the twenty-first century not text?"

He headed for a bar made of dark mahogany and glossy black marble along the far wall. "Sunshine, I do all my interacting with women live and in the flesh." He lifted a bottle of chardonnay from the rack, removed the cork and set the wine on the counter, meeting her gaze. "If I want to ask her out, I speak to her in person. If I'm going to be late for a date, I call her on the phone." He pulled a beer from the refrigerator, twisted off the cap with a hissing pop, and shot her a skeptical look. "I do not spend 24/7 with a cellular attached to my hand so that I can inform my friends via Twitter that I'm leaving for the store to buy a six pack of beer." He flipped the cap with his fingers, and it hit the garbage can with a ping.

She bit back a smile. "That's good, because I doubt anyone is interested in those kinds of details." She wasn't sure whether she was making headway with him. After a pause, she pulled down a wineglass from the hanging rack over the marble counter and poured herself some chardonnay. She sat at the bar and sent him a measured look. "Cutter, I'm not asking you to provide the public with a banal running commentary on every detail of your life."

Beer in hand, Cutter rounded the counter and climbed onto the stool beside her, planting his elbows on the bar. "So my search for just the right toilet paper isn't relevant."

Jessica couldn't help herself. She smiled. "No."

He swiveled in his seat to face her. "What about those annoying little emoticons?" A faint frown appeared. "Smiley faces aren't my style."

"I've noticed. And the double smiley faces are definitely out. Though there is one for a devilish grin that would work really well for you."

"I could do a devilish grin." He demonstrated one on his face.

She subdued the laugh that threatened to surface. "LOLs and exclamation points aren't a requirement either."

"What about using all caps?"

"Caps are for amateurs."

He leaned forward a touch. "What if I have something important to do? Like turning a woman's head with my sparkling wit and personality? Wouldn't I want to capitalize the word *beautiful* when I compliment her on her looks?"

The intensity in his eyes made it clear he was talking about her. A low burn started, but she ignored it. "Forget the looks. You'd win more points complimenting her on her sense of humor. And a sophisticated texter doesn't need the caps button." She tipped her head. "He leaves a woman weak in the knees with just the right words."

The hint of a smile appeared on his face. "A real man leaves a woman weak in the knees with just the right *look*."

Absolutely. Which was why it was a good thing she was sitting down. Because he was sending out some potent, powerful vibes. She was almost tempted to be charmed. She took a fortifying sip of crisp, dry wine, eyeing him warily over her glass.

"I'll agree to go through with this if you lend me a hand in the beginning," he said.

"What do you mean?"

"We get together and you share my texting responsibilities."

She coughed on her wine, the words sputtering out in a squeak. "You want me to flirt with other women for you?"

"Just help me out until I get going."

"Absolutely not." She turned to face him in her seat. "You have to do your own flirting."

"Why? I'm not marrying any of them. I'm not even agreeing to date them. All I'm promising is one lousy dinner in the name of a good cause."

"Because it's…because it's…" as her mouth grappled to catch up with her brain, Jessica's mind scrambled for the right word. *Sacrilegious* sounded melodramatic. *Rude* he clearly wouldn't care about. At a loss, she set her glass down with a clink. "Because it's unromantic, not to mention unethical. You cannot outsource your flirting."

He tipped his head in disbelief. "Jessica, we're not talking about destroying our local economy."

"You're the Wildcard," she said levelly. "Women elude security and pick locks to climb into your bed. I'm sure you're more than qualified to handle a little internet flirting with several women at the same time."

Unimpressed by her attempts at flattery, Cutter said, "I've never had to flirt with a woman online in my life." He gave a small shrug. "It's either have some help to get me started or I won't do it."

Jessica propped her elbows on the counter and covered her eyes with her palms. Cutter Thompson was frustrating and cynical. But she'd promised Steve.

She *owed* Steve.

He might not have been the love of her life as she'd once hoped, but he'd helped her find her passion. The great gift of career satisfaction. She loved her work. It defined her. And, despite their divorce, Steve had been a big part of that discovery. And his advice during her fledgling business years had been invaluable.

She wouldn't be the success she was today with his support.

"Fine." She dropped her hands to the counter and turned her head to meet Cutter's gaze. "But here are the rules. Once you get the hang of it, I'm done. And no one can know I'm helping you. They have to believe that everything comes from you or the whole thing crumbles in a heap of shame. Maintaining the integrity of the event is my top priority."

The expression on his face promised nothing. "I want to have my 'Cuda done by the end of the month. That's my priority."

With a sense of victory and relief, Cutter pulled open the glass door and entered the small but elegant reception room of Perfect Pair Inc., pulling off his baseball cap and sunglasses. It had taken twenty minutes to shake the reporter trailing him since he'd left his house. A full week of media hype about the fundraiser had the worst of Miami's parasitic paparazzi on a renewed quest to hunt Cutter Thompson down. He'd left North Carolina and moved back to Miami to avoid this kind of scrutiny.

Of course, his sudden aversion to interviews only made the press hungrier for tidbits of his activities, but he was determined to keep the facts about his memory loss private. Bad enough he'd regained consciousness in the ambulance in the worst agony of his life; no need for the world to rehash every gritty detail. He refused to tap dance his way around another grilling over what was next for Cutter Thompson. And he sure as hell wouldn't field one more question about his reason for illegally bumping Chester Coon.

Hell, when—*if*—he ever figured out the answers, he'd take out a flippin' full-page ad in the *Times* and let everyone know.

Until then, every member of the press was persona non grata in Cutter's book.

Even though he'd managed to lose the newshound tailing him, the encounter had left him with a foul mood he couldn't shake. He'd been having a good day in the garage. The pain was tolerable, and the new camshaft went in like a dream.

But then he'd had to take a trip across town with a bloodsucker on his trail. And he owed his ramped-up publicity appeal to do-gooder Jessica Wilson—the lady who'd toppled his plans for seclusion with a barrage of sympathy-invoking photos.

Weak. He was well and truly weak.

His only option now was to get in and out as quickly as possible. Complete the first round of chatting with his contestants and get back to the peace of his garage. He needed to crawl back under the 'Cuda. Solving problems there was simple. Things connected and made sense. Broken parts could be easily repaired or replaced.

Unlike his life.

With a frown, he scanned his surroundings. The small reception room off to the left was decorated like a cozy living area, complete with a collection of leather couches arranged in a circle, the walls lined with pictures of smiling couples mocking his black mood. Some looked candid, some were professionally done, and others were wedding photos of happy brides and grooms.

He grimaced at the marital bliss propaganda being displayed on the wall.

Jessica appeared in the hallway, her lovely long legs bare beneath a gray skirt that ended in a dainty ruffle. A gauzy pink blouse clung to gentle curves. She was an intriguing mix of sophisticated class, professionalism and soft femininity. But she believed in true love and things like 'effective communication.'

"Thanks for coming here," Jessica said. "I have to meet someone for dinner at eight, so I'm pressed for time."

Yet, here she was, championing her cause. Helping him do his part. He was still trying to figure that one out. "Why is this fundraiser so important to you? Was your childhood so awful you feel obligated to fix it for others?"

Her expression was one of restraint, with a hint of annoyance. "No. My childhood consisted of two parents who loved and nurtured me. I'm a longtime supporter of the work the Brice Foundation does, and my ex-husband is chairman of the board. I promised him I'd recruit you for the benefit dinner."

His eyebrows lifted. That she was divorced came as a surprise. That she was still on speaking terms with her ex was a shock. "Seems strange to hear the words *help* and *ex-husband* in the same sentence."

"This is the twenty-first century, Mr. Thompson," she said as she started down a hallway.

He followed beside her. "So you keep telling me."

"Our marriage failed," she said. "But our friendship didn't. And I owe him."

Owe?

Growing up in his world meant divorced parents who talked about each other with animosity and refused to speak to one another. Which had left a five-year-old Cutter carrying messages between them…because they couldn't get along for the two minutes it took to discuss his visitations. By all reports, his parents had been head-over-heels in love until his mom had got knocked up with Cutter and they'd had to tie the knot. According to his mother, for the entire four years of her marriage, bliss had been a distant memory.

Who needed that kind of misery?

He hiked an eyebrow dryly. "What's with the sense of obligation toward your ex? Did you treat him like crap during your marriage?"

She shot him a cutting look. "I owe him because he helped me start my online dating service after our divorce."

Cutter came to a halt and watched her continue down the hall. "So your *ex-husband* helped you start a business finding love for other people?" It was hard enough comprehending how a woman so thoroughly indoctrinated in the happily-ever-after club could have joined the till-divorce-do-us-part league. But the irony of her profession was comical. "Shouldn't a failed marriage disqualify you from the job?"

She stopped and turned to face him, a frown on her face, her voice firm. "A divorce doesn't disqualify you from anything."

He moved closer to her, puzzlement pulling his eyebrows higher. "Ruining your own life wasn't good enough, you feel the need to make others miserable, too?"

She actually bit her lower lip. Cutter was sure it was to cut off a sharp retort, and he was amazed she managed to sound so civil. "When two people are compatible, marriage isn't miserable." She turned into an office clearly decorated for a woman, done in soft mauves and creams. "And despite my divorce, I still believe in romantic relationships."

Cutter followed her inside, letting out an amused scoff. "I'm not divorced, and even I know they're a crock."

She rounded her leather-topped desk adorned with a vase of cheerful yellow lilies and took a seat at her computer, eyeing him warily. Her tone held more than a trace of concern. "Mr. Thompson," she said. "Let's try not to bring up your jaded views while discussing your ideal date online." It seemed she'd concluded he was a hopeless cause.

Hell yeah. Count him up as one who had seen the light a long time ago.

"My views aren't jaded," he said. "They're realistic." And the sooner the two of them got started, the sooner he could be done with this fake flirt fest. "Okay. How do we start?"

"With a question for the contestants. Something to get the conversation going."

"About dating, right?" He crossed to stop behind her chair and frowned at the waiting computer, feeling foolish for getting involved. Cutter hoped the sullen teenage Emmanuel wound up a friggin' Supreme Court Justice. Nothing less would justify caving in to this absurd unreality show. "How about asking their favorite date destination?"

Jessica folded her arms across her chest. "You need something more open-ended. All someone has to say is the beach or a restaurant and the conversation dies."

"At least I'd be done for the evening. And you'd have time for a pre-dinner drink."

Jessica looked up at him with a determined pair of brown Bambi eyes that said she'd miss the dinner before she'd do less than her best.

Her ex must be one hell of a guy.

With a resigned sigh, Cutter sat on her desk. "Okay, what if I ask them about their worst dating experiences?"

"Same problem. Those require individual responses and you're looking for an interactive debate." A small grimace filled her face. "Not to mention it's a negative way to start."

He stared at her. "You mean, not only do I have to have this debate, I have to be *upbeat* about it?" He didn't know how, not since he was a kid when his dad had left for good and his mother had blamed Cutter.

Not a lot to be upbeat about there.

"Number-one rule of first dates," Jessica said with a soothing smile, but he had the feeling she was faking it. Somehow, that made it all the more intriguing. "No one likes a whiner."

He wasn't sure why, but he found her amusing. "I thought it was don't eat anything with garlic and wear comfortable clothes."

For a brief moment, she almost looked horrified. "Your

clothes should make a *statement*. They are a reflection of you."

"True," he said matter-of-factly. "You can tell a lot about a woman by the underwear she wears."

With a sigh, she raised an eyebrow dryly, her tone carefully patient. "By the time you get to her underwear, you should know quite a bit about her already."

He shook his head. "You go for pastel colors. Lace. No thongs. Nothing see-through. Practical, yet pretty. And not too racy."

A hint of color appeared on her cheeks, but her tone was defiant. "Have you thought of a question for your contestants yet?"

Cutter rubbed his jaw, enjoying her flushed face. "I take it favorite lingerie choices are out?"

Her answer was a slight narrowing of her eyes and an expression of forbearance that was downright adorable, and Cutter realized his foul mood was long gone. Damn, when had he started enjoying himself? And how could someone so ridiculously optimistic about relationships pull him out of his funk with her militant views on dating? He pulled his gaze from her caramel eyes and tried to concentrate on the task at hand, staring at the blank screen.

Cupid's longest-running gag was torturing mankind with the opposites-attract rule.

The thought inspired him. "How about—*What creates a spark between two people?*"

He knew he'd succeeded when the light in her eyes flickered brighter. And the admiration on her face was worth waiting for. "Perfect," she said, her bone-melting smile of approval skewering his insides.

Jessica turned to the computer and typed. A few moments later, she looked up, her dark, exotic gaze on him. "Love Potion Number Nine's reply: *chemistry.* What do you want to say in response?"

Caught in her spell, and captivated by her sooty lashes, he had no idea. "What happened to love potions number one through eight?"

"You can't mock her user name."

"Is that first-date rule number two?"

"No," she said dryly. "It's just assumed under the one about negative whiners."

His lips twitched, itching to grin, but he persevered. "You sure have a lot of dating rules." He forced his gaze from chocolate eyes to the monitor. "Ask her to define chemistry."

As Jessica entered his question, another contestant's answer popped onto the screen, and Cutter leaned forward to read it. "Calamity Jane says spark is defined by sexual attraction."

That was a no-brainer. He looked down at Jessica again, her sweetly spiced scent tantalizing him while her smoky eyes eroded his need for distance. Not only was she beautiful, she was feisty without getting too defensive. Sensual, and confident in her sexuality without being desperate.

Used to be, getting in the zone could only be achieved by high speeds. That feeling of intense focus, a heightened awareness and being both mentally and physically in tune with his body. Now, one look from the beautiful Jessica Wilson and he was in the zone.

And how could he be so attracted to an optimistic, self-styled guru on relationships?

Because he was definitely in tune with his body. Maybe *too* in tune.

Blood pumped through his veins, disturbing in its intensity. "I'd say Calamity is on to something," he murmured. "No discussion necessary. I'll just agree with her."

Her eyelids flared in panic. "You can't."

"Why not?"

"First of all, if you agree then there's no give and take. No debate is boring. Second of all, spark isn't defined simply by sexual attraction. The physical is just a small part. Chemistry is a connection based on shared interests."

Amused, Cutter hiked a brow. "Unless we're talking about a shared interest in each other's bodies, that's not what Calamity Jane said."

The pink mouth went flat. "Calamity is wrong."

As Cutter looked down at her, the urge to smile was now almost overwhelming. "Now who's being negative?" From this angle, he noticed her blouse gapped at the neckline, and the curves of her breasts were cupped in a lacy bra.

He was right, except it was light purple, not pink. Lavender and lace.

Ms. Sunshine was wearing a cliché.

Delight spread through him. He'd changed his mind. Suffering the disruption of his day, enduring the bloodsucking journalist's chase, both were worth her company.

"Back to Calamity," Jessica said. "Why don't we start with this for a response—*Sexual attraction is important.*" She looked up at him. "What should we add?" Her beautiful gaze looked thoughtful.

A pair of eyes that could make a guy willingly trade his man cave for an evening in a mauve-colored, foo-foo office peddling romance online.

He sent her a faint grin. "How about…*I also like a woman who challenges me.*"

Her smile was like healing salve on a burn. "That's better."

Yes…it was. Cutter's grin grew more defined. "Oh, and tell her I also have a thing for lavender-and-lace underwear."

CHAPTER THREE

DISASTER.

The fundraiser for the Brice Foundation was going to be a monstrous disaster, and it was all her fault.

Stopping for a red light, Jessica glanced at her watch. She only had ten minutes to get to her dinner date. The past hour had been long, frustrating and infinitely illuminating, and she was amazed she hadn't pulled out every hair on her head.

And, as if Cutter's attitude alone wasn't enough, he'd looked down her shirt. Like an impulsive twelve-year-old riding a testosterone high he couldn't control. Granted, from his angle on her desk it would have been hard to prevent. But still, mentioning what he saw was less than gallant.

The word *gallant* had no business existing in the same universe as Cutter Thompson.

In the beginning, she'd been less than thrilled to continue her involvement with Cutter during his Battle of the Sexes participation. Now it seemed it was a blessing in disguise.

Because Cutter Thompson in a stock car was sure to get a woman's heart racing.

Cutter Thompson in a TV interview was truly electric.

But Cutter Thompson flirting online was a catastrophe.

Every time a contestant responded, his automatic response would have alienated half the participants and a good portion of Miami as well. He didn't appreciate that a cocky response—where the words weren't tempered with a handsome face, green eyes that sparkled with humor and a teasing tone—could have disastrous effects.

In retrospect, maybe she should have realized the pitfalls of asking ASCAR's former number-one driver to participate. When she'd offered to do this stunt for Steve it was to help make it a success, not steep it in shame. And Steve had been right. She should have gone for the local cello player who had won the North American Academy of Musicians' competition last year. So he'd been a little soft and a bit too sweet. No one would have noticed online.

Now she was stuck with the Wildcard, Master of the Cutting Comment.

And how many years had he been honing that ability to whip out a blithe insult with stunning clarity, just skirting the edges of amusing charm?

Jessica turned her car into a parking space at the restaurant, cut off the engine, and sat, tapping her fingernails on the steering wheel. The Battle of the Sexes was a month long, and she didn't want to hover over the man and deflect his every inappropriate remark for the entire competition. Which meant Mr. Cutter Thompson needed a lesson or two in how to behave online. He was way beyond help in his personal, face-to-face interactions, but if she could just get him through the publicity stunt, the rest didn't matter. After she was done with him, he could insult the Pope if he wanted.

Tomorrow when they met for round two, she was going to review online etiquette and the rules of acceptable behavior. Surely the man was trainable.

If he wasn't, she'd have to spend the next month glued to his side, fending off furtive peeks at her underwear. And the thought of that was far from appealing.

"Nice job, Jess," Steve said, his voice muffled. One hand on the steering wheel, Jessica adjusted the earpiece of her cell phone, and Steve's words were clearer when he went on. "Last night's Cutter Thompson debut was pure gold. Is he a prima donna to work with?"

Prima donna? Her fingers clenched the wheel. More like a cross between a prima donna and a raging hormonal teen. And he wielded a masculinity that would make him millions if it were bottled and sold. Actually, it had—Jessica had enjoyed the perverse pleasure of eating her breakfast this morning while staring at Cutter in his racing uniform, arms crossed, his trademark suggestion of a grin plastered on her cereal box. And for the love of God, why couldn't he just *smile?* It was as if he knew his hint at a grin was more powerful than the beaming smile of a Hollywood leading man.

"He was a little difficult. But I was ready for him," she said, feeling guilty for lying. How could anyone ever be ready for the likes of Cutter?

"No one is ever more prepared than you," Steve said. "And speaking of, how did your dinner go last night?"

Jessica made a face as she turned the car into Cutter's neighborhood. "He was certainly nothing like his online dating profile."

"There are a lot of weirdos out there." Steve's voice grew concerned. "You're steering clear of the stalkers, right?"

Jessica smiled. "No stalkers yet."

"Good. But if you need me to hire a hitman to break some knees, just let me know."

"A true sign of a good friend."

Steve paused before he went on. "I just want to see you happy, Jess."

Jessica gripped the wheel harder, and signed off, disconnecting her cellular.

She *was* happy. And one day she'd find someone to share that happiness with. Because he was out there. She could feel it. The perfect man for her. It was like she told her customers at Perfect Pairs…

"You have to be open to love to find it. And you have to be willing to work hard, before *and* after you do."

Steve was a great guy; he just hadn't been the right guy. And all the hard work in the world couldn't overcome a mismatched choice. The blues threatened to color her mood, and she swatted them back.

For now, it didn't matter anyway. Her life, full with running her business, had taken on a bursting-at-the-seams quality since she'd dragged Cutter into the fundraiser. For a little while, dating would have to take a backseat.

And she'd learned a lot from her mistakes; next time she was positive she'd get it right. Then again, as a child she'd been positive her parents were happy, too, and look how wrong she'd been about that. She ignored the dull ache in her heart, the pain an unwelcome guest she'd learned to live with.

She pulled into the driveway of Cutter's modern three-story home, hidden from the street by a jungle of thick, woody banyan trees and patches of bamboo. A yard as wild as the owner itself. The garage constituted the entire first level, and on the door was a note: *Come Around Back.*

After rounding the house, Jessica passed a sparkling blue pool and headed down the grassy, palm-tree-studded backyard that ended at Biscayne Bay. A powerful-looking speedboat was parked at the dock, and Cutter was on deck, coiling a rope with easy, confident movements.

She crossed to the end of the dock. His brown hair had streaks of gold that glinted in the sunshine. In khaki shorts and a knit shirt, he made casual cool.

"You look like you're feeling better," she said.

"I'm waiting on a part for the 'Cuda, so I spent the day tuning up the boat. I figured we could take a test run and woo my contestants at the same time." His sea-green eyes roamed down her peach princess-styled dress to her two-inch sandals. "But you look overdressed."

"Much like blood, silk is always in style."

A twinkle appeared in his eyes as he held out his hand. "Then climb aboard."

As he helped her onto the boat, the skin-on-skin touch was more disturbing than she'd prepared for. Perhaps she simply needed to acclimate to the sight of bare, muscular legs. "Nice boat," she said, carefully removing her fingers from his.

"With a four-hundred-and-thirty-horsepower engine, she's one of the fastest crafts in the neighborhood."

Jessica settled onto the leather bench that stretched across the stern, resting her arms along the back. This was one element of Cutter Thompson she was equipped to deal with. "That's because your neighborhood is full of wimpy vessels."

From the bucket seat in front of her, hand on the key in the ignition, Cutter turned to shoot her a look. "Are you saying my equipment is small?"

She smiled and crossed her legs. He was defending his boat the way he'd defended his car. He was such a *guy*. "I'm telling you your equipment is *slow*."

"Sunshine—" he hooked his arm on the back of his chair "—nothing about me is slow." He lifted his brows. "Including my boat."

"I've driven faster."

His face exuded skepticism. "What boat would that be?"

"A Mach III Sidewinder."

He stared at her, the chiseled, masculine planes of his face lit by the sun. Finally, he let out a reverent whistle. "Damn. Those top out at a hundred and seventy miles per hour."

"I know. My father builds them." And after her parents' divorce, she'd spent hours with her father at his plant, her life divided evenly between two worlds. One ultra-feminine, the other pure male.

"I suppose my plan to impress you with speed won't work," he said.

"I'm afraid not."

Suddenly, his mouth held the potential for a smile, but even skirting the edge of possibility he managed to leave her breathless. "Guess I'll have to come up with something better." His look brimmed with cocky promise.

Stunned, Jessica realized her heart was thumping in her ribs. Cutter's mesmerizing gaze released hers when he turned to start the boat and eased them out into the channel, where she finally inhaled a breath of salty, fresh air. The sun was warm, and, without his focus on her, she was able to relax. But since when was she even fleetingly susceptible to Neanderthals?

She pushed the thought aside as they cruised past exclusive homes with tropical landscapes, private boats aligned in a parade of wealth, under bridges, and finally through downtown. Columns of condominiums and skyscrapers dwarfed them, stainless-steel-and-glass giants gleaming in the sun.

After finding a safe spot with a view of the city, Cutter cut the engine and tossed out the anchor, taking a seat beside her. He propped his legs up on the edge of the boat, the extension of hard muscle seemingly going on forever.

Yes, it had to be the naked limbs that were getting under her skin.

But she was here to complete her task, not gawk at powerful legs dusted with dark hair. Jessica sat up a little higher and forced her gaze to his face. But the square-cut jaw, green eyes and brown hair with touches of gold were striking in a wholly masculine way. Not exactly the visual relief she needed. Jessica cleared her throat, reining in her reaction. "We need to discuss social-networking etiquette."

The grimace on his beautiful face was absolute. "I'd rather you pull out my fingernails."

She went on, ignoring his lack of enthusiasm. "You need

to remember that your words minus the facial expression and the inflection in your tone are open to interpretation." Holding his gaze, she used her tone to emphasize her point. "You think you're being charming and witty, and the recipient thinks you're being insulting."

"Most of the time I am."

She stared at him and realized he was telling the truth. Why would someone go out of their way to be disagreeable? "Well...that won't work for us."

"I don't know how to be a suck-up."

She held back the lift of her brow at the understatement. "Just be aware of the subtle nuances in your words and how they can be interpreted."

"Nuances?" he said, as if the word had a foreign taste.

"And remember," she said, continuing her usual spiel on online interactions, pleased he was at least pretending to listen—even if her every statement was followed by a sarcastic comment. "People are interested in those who are interested in *them*. A little self-deprecating humor is good, as it's humanizing, but not too much or you'll appear to lack self-confidence." Of course, this piece of advice hardly applied to Cutter Thompson. But she was offering up her full speech, because this man needed all the help he could get.

His brows drew together in doubt. "Maybe I should have agreed to establish peace in the Middle East instead," Cutter said. "Might have been easier." He settled deeper into the bench. "But I did manage to come up with today's question for my contestants—*If I invited you to a costume party, which superhero pair would you want to go as and why?*"

Jessica smiled. Impressive progress. Mr. Thompson appeared to be trainable. Maybe after today's session he could carry this off on his own. "I like it. It has humor, a flirtatious quality and requires more than a one-word answer." Feeling encouraged, Jessica pulled her phone from her purse. "I'll send it out now."

"No need." Cutter retrieved his cellular from his shorts and went to work, his thumbs clumsily pushing the buttons.

She blinked. "I thought you didn't text."

"I spent the day practicing." He met her gaze. "Gave my old pit crew buddies a blow-by-blow account on the tune-up of my boat."

Jessica's mouth twitched in a smile, trying to picture a bunch of men, hands smeared with grease, phones beeping in their back pockets. "And what did they think?"

"That I'd gone off my rocker." By his tone and the look on his face, she could tell he agreed with their assessment.

"It's a quick way to send out a message," she said. "It's also perfect for when I don't have time for one of my mother's lengthy conversations." She sent him a dry smile. "You might find it useful with your family."

The lines of skepticism vanished from his face and Cutter looked to the city. Staring across the glistening urban landscape, he went on in an even tone. "I don't have a family."

Jessica's heart did a double take. "Where are your parents?"

"My dad took off when I was a kid and my mom died five years ago."

His tone was matter-of-fact, and held no trace of emotion.

"I'm sorry," she said quietly.

"Don't be." His tone was easy, and the small twist of his lips didn't betray a hint of lingering sadness. "The Thompson mantra is when life sucks, deal with it."

Which had served him well, no doubt. She studied his profile thoughtfully, wondering how old he'd been when he'd adopted the attitude.

When he turned to look at her, he must have caught the question in her eyes. "Sunshine," he said with a light scoff as he sent her an amused look. "I don't have any feelings to share and I don't do Dr. Phil. If you're looking for a man with a feminine side…" He leaned in, bringing his hot, sea-green eyes and bold gaze so close that her breath momentarily froze in her throat. "You're looking at the wrong guy."

She was looking all right. Despite the rising rate of her heart, and now her breathing, she resisted the need to break eye contact. As she stared at Cutter, her brain frantically broadcast a warning about their incompatibility. Unfortunately, her body wasn't picking up the signal.

Because when it came to men, she preferred charm. And she insisted on polite. Or—for the love of God—at least *agreeable*.

None of which described Cutter Thompson. But when his gaze dropped to her mouth, as if contemplating kissing her, the rate of her breathing dropped to zero.

He'd take what he wanted with no apologies. No slow, sensual lead-ups. No rose petals on silk sheets. And she was unfamiliar with the rebel breed. Steve had been her first lover, and what had started out gentle had grown into comfortable fun. The sex, at least, had been good. And she'd entered into two intimate relationships since her divorce. Satisfying, both, but not the kind that lit the world and left scorch marks on the ground.

And not one of the men wore the raw edges that defined Cutter.

Water lapped the boat as they stared at each other until his phone beeped. Cutter glanced at the small screen, breaking the spell, and Jessica quietly sucked in air, relieved with the fresh supply of oxygen again.

"Calamity Jane says she wants to go as Batman and Batgirl because I'd look good in tights." Cutter shot her a lazy, brash look. "Guess I'll have to explain that real men would choose the sexy, villainous Catwoman over the friends-with-predictably-boring-benefits Batgirl every time."

Jessica didn't bother stifling her groan. So much for progress.

Lovely, his self-centered ways went beyond money, they

applied to women, too. She shouldn't have been surprised, but his flippant attitude towards relationships went against every value she held dear.

His smoldering glance…the bold stare… No doubt he delivered that look to every woman he found attractive. Cutter Thompson was the worst of the worst, a man with the emotional depth of a flatworm and a derisive attitude toward romance. He didn't believe in The One, more like The Many. He was everything she *didn't* want, wrapped up in a package that was oh-so-much worse. And if the rate of her thumping heart was any indication, her body's reaction was about more than naked, muscular legs.

Which meant she wasn't quite as immune to the egocentric bad boy as she'd thought.

An hour later Cutter watched Jessica maneuver the boat towards home. She'd taken over the helm so he could continue his instant messaging, and he was impressed with her ability to handle the craft and intercept his inappropriate comments at the same time. The more appalled her look, the more he'd enjoyed himself. And although peace and quiet had been his only goal since the day he'd announced his retirement, Jessica Wilson had fast and furiously become a major exception to the rule.

He should find Emmanuel, the teenager with the bad-ass photographic attitude, and thank him personally.

She was too easy to tease. "I think I have the hang of this online flirting thing," he said. "I don't need your help anymore."

Jessica stared at him, wide-eyed, and with more than a trace of fear.

A small grin slipped past before he could stop it. He hadn't smiled this much since he'd first won Nationals. "What?" he said with as much innocence as a thirty-year-old washed-up race-car driver could muster. "You don't trust me?"

She skillfully maneuvered alongside his dock and cut the engine. "I absolutely trust you to alienate Susie Q Public."

After hopping out, he secured the boat, and then hiked a brow at Jessica. "Women know better than to look for Prince Charming in me." He liked how she managed to maintain her femininity while commenting on the oil level in his car or parking a boat with finesse. "That's why they find me so attractive. It's a primal propagation-of-the-species thing." Cutter leaned in, took Jessica's hand and helped her onto the dock beside him. Her ethereally lovely face and mysterious scent entwined around his senses. "Deep down they know that nice guys finish last." He'd learned that the same way he'd learned everything else. The hard way. And early on.

"Nice guys do *not* finish last." Her doe-eyed brown gaze held his. "And if you don't mind, I'll hang around and moderate the Cutter Thompson mouth until this nightmare of a flirting debacle is over."

He almost grinned again. Much more of this and he'd lose his reputation. "Don't mind at all."

Jessica looked as if it wouldn't matter if he did. Cutter was still contemplating smiling in amusement when she continued. "Don't forget the cocktail party at the Miami Aquarium on Saturday. Steve invited reporters to the mixer so the media will have access to our Battle of the Sexes celebrities. It should help increase our press coverage."

Media, reporters and press coverage—hell no.

The idea left a nasty taste in his mouth, and his jaw muscles hardened, all thoughts of smiling gone. "I have no intention of attending a party with journalists." Fun time was over. Time to get back to the 'Cuda. He'd find something else to work on until the new carburetor arrived.

Cutter headed toward the house, and Jessica fell into step beside him. "It's not a press conference," she said. "Just a couple of reporters from a few of the major papers will be in attendance."

Sure, the same journalists who had been staking out his house since he'd returned to Miami. Cutter was better at losing them now, but no way was he gonna *choose* to be in the same room with the press.

"I have no interest in interviews," he said. "The last thing I want is a hotshot reporter grilling me about my dating methods and writing an exposé on my social life." He knew damn well that wasn't what they'd ask. They'd use the Battle of the Sexes publicity stunt as an excuse to get close and then badger him hard about the accident.

A tumultuous riot of tension and nerves broke out in his body.

Jessica slowly came to a stop and stared at him, looking baffled. "You never seemed to worry about the media's opinion before."

He halted on the walkway. "That was when dealing with them went with the job description."

When the questions had been easy to answer and the banter had been full of fun and camaraderie. Lately all the banter had been replaced by hard-core grilling about his wreck, his *reason* for the rash move that ended his career. And he was no closer to knowing the answer now than he had been two months ago.

He might never remember the moment he'd screwed up his life.

His gut roiled, and his gaze locked with hers. "No cocktail party. No schmoozing with the press." He frowned and continued up the walk, heading for his garage. "And no changing my mind."

The next morning Jessica ate her breakfast, flipping through the morning paper as Cutter's picture stared at her from her cereal box. She had yet to figure out how the man could have such an effect on her.

Handsome, yes.

Virile, most definitely.

But what did it matter when he was the antithesis of everything she was looking for?

In the five years since her divorce, she'd been on a lot of first dates, had been subjected to every possible combination of good looks and charm imaginable. She'd even gone to dinner with a model who regularly appeared in *GQ* magazine. He was drop-dead gorgeous and sweet, but the chemistry during the evening was flat. They had nothing in common. When he asked her out for a second date, she'd politely turned him down.

She'd thought she was impervious to the sexual appeal of an unsuitable guy, yet the powerful pull of Cutter Thompson was proving greater than the sum total of her experiences.

With a sigh, Jessica flipped to the society section of the morning newspaper and spied the front-page photo, a bolt of shock zipping along her nerves. Her spoonful of granola hovered in the air as she scanned the picture of her and Cutter. They were sitting side by side in the boat, Cutter texting on his cellular, and Jessica leaning in to look at his message. But the headline was the worst part—Is Local Racing Hero Turned Recluse Now Dating?

Shock turned to horror as she read the accompanying blurb, mostly about Cutter's refusal to appear in public since retiring. And whoever had snapped the photo had done their homework, accurately identifying her. They'd even mentioned her motto at Perfect Pair: Fostering honest dialogue in finding The One. Multiple questions regarding their relationship were raised in the paragraph, suggesting she and Cutter were hot and heavy into an affair.

Panic spread and, without a second thought, she grabbed her purse and headed out the door.

Twenty minutes later Jessica stepped out of her car and onto Cutter's driveway. The garage door was open, and rock music blared. After she passed through the entrance, she switched off the music and headed toward the old muscle car and the pair of tennis shoes protruding from beneath.

Balancing on the balls of her feet, she squatted and leaned forward, staring up past long legs, a flat abdomen, to arms that jutted into the underbelly of the vehicle. "Cutter, we have a problem."

He kept right on tinkering. "I'm gonna start thinking you don't like my taste in music."

Jessica summoned her patience and tried again. "Cutter, our picture was in the paper."

His hand continued torquing the wrench. "So?"

With an exasperated sigh, Jessica reached down and pulled on Cutter's feet, rolling him from beneath the vehicle in a smooth motion.

Flat on his back, Cutter stared up at her, the wrench still clutched in his hand. After a brief pause, Cutter said, "I gather it wasn't a flattering photograph."

"It shows the two of us texting together."

A doubtful frown appeared. "And again I say…*so?*"

Jessica covered her eyes with her palm and counted, but only made it to seven. "Cutter," she said as calmly as she could, dropping her hand. "This doesn't look good for our contest. What if someone guesses I'm helping you? And even if they don't come to that conclusion, if you *were* seriously dating me as the paper suggested, then you shouldn't be flirting with other women online."

Her words triggered a skeptical lift of his brow. "Not all of us hold ourselves to the same restrictions."

Lips pressed flat, she ignored the temptation to comment on his unromantic morals and went on. "Okay, forget that you're a lost cause. But you agreed to the rules, remember? Like the one that stated you would keep your relationships private until the contest was over. Image is important. And how will it look to my customers if I'm dating a man who is flirting with other women? Or worse, if I'm *helping* him flirt with other women." Panic filled her chest, and her palms grew damp. "My business is built on the belief that you can find a soul mate through honest communication."

"Sunshine, too much honest communication will kill your matchmaking attempts." A still-skeptical eyebrow eased higher, though his tone grew thoughtful. "And I never could understand how the word *soul* got linked to the enjoyable act of *mating*."

"Cutter." Her voice was sharp. "This isn't about your hopelessly warped views."

He blew out a sigh and lowered his wrench. "Okay. Help me sit up so I can have this torturous conversation without the physical pain as well."

Jessica grasped his hand and helped him into a sitting position. His fingers were warm, the calluses rough against her palm, and the blaze sweeping through her body was heating her from the inside out. She braced her feet and provided support as he rose.

All six foot three of his muscular frame towered over her, and he stood way too close for reasonable heart rates. The telltale suggestion of a grin returned. "I must be healing. That didn't hurt at all."

Yes it had. And it still did, because his musky scent was tempting. Jessica frowned, annoyed by her pounding heart. "Too bad." Because if he dropped dead right now all her problems would be solved.

His lips twitched. Well, he might think the situation was funny, but this year's Battle of the Sexes was her creation. And her business meant the world to her. Bringing people companionship, finding The One for others is what sustained her hope that, someday, she would find the guy for her. "The public cannot think we are dating. Not when it could put the contest and my business at stake. Perception *is* reality."

"The public doesn't give a rat's ass what you do in private. And for all anyone knows, we're just good friends who went out for a boat ride while following some movie star on Twitter."

Frustrated by his teasing tone, Jessica closed her eyes and inhaled and exhaled—twice. "I know you think my job is ridiculous." She lifted her lids. "I *know* you think true love is a crock. But this is what I do." The rising panic made her voice tight. "This is who I am. And if I ruin my reputation, it could have serious repercussions for my business."

A frown appeared as he blew out a breath. "I don't want you to ruin your business either," he said. He ruffled a hand through his hair, a look of resignation on his face. "You have a wall full of grateful customers. And I respect that."

"Thank you." She blinked back the budding tears of frustrated relief, stunned by his words. "But that still doesn't solve my problem."

His face thoughtful, Cutter crossed to the car and leaned his back against the door, folding his arms across his chest. The distance was nice, but his biceps bulged beneath his T-shirt and, for a brief second, Jessica lost her train of thought.

"What did it say?" he asked

Blinking, Jessica tried to focus. "What did what say?"

"The paper."

"It mentioned your reclusive status, who I was, my business, and then it questioned our relationship."

He studied her thoughtfully for a moment, rubbing the back of his neck. "Damn," he muttered, and her anxiety winched higher as he went on. He dropped his arm to his side. "I know what to do."

Jessica suppressed the urge to grab his shirt and shake him to spill the goods. The look on his face spoke volumes. Whatever his plan, he wasn't happy about it.

"You go to the Aquarium with a date and I'll go alone," he said, his voice grim. "An evening with the two of us at the same party—but clearly not as a couple—will support the theory that we're just friends."

Jessica held his gaze as the full implication of his words washed over her. He was offering to go to the party. Attending a function that included the media. One he had adamantly refused to participate in before.

Cutter Thompson wasn't the completely selfish bastard she'd thought.

Gratitude flooded, overriding her good sense, and she launched herself forward, throwing her arms around his chest for a hug. She landed against a wall of warm steel that smelled of musk and man, momentarily paralyzing everything but her pulse, every particle in her body aware of Cutter at a primal, cellular level.

Cutter's voice was strained, as if in pain. "No need to get mushy. It's not like I asked you to marry me."

Jessica released a small laugh; intense relief over her business, mixed with an armful of potent male, was making her uncharacteristically giddy. "Quit being an idiot, Cutter. I appreciate what you're doing for me." She dropped her arms and stepped back, ordering her heart to ease its pace. Though her body still pulsed, her gaze never wavered. "And I would never say yes to a proposal from you."

His expression mixed a grimace with amusement. "No need to worry, Sunshine." The rare but devilish almost-grin returned. "I'd never ask."

CHAPTER FOUR

THE sprawling lobby of the Miami Aquarium was dotted with twinkling lights, huge tanks of colorful, exotic fish, and people in elegant finery. Phillip Carr, CEO of Carr Investments, looked as if he'd been born into this world wearing an expensive tuxedo. He had blond hair, blue eyes and a smile so smooth it warranted its own flavor of ice cream. But as far as Cutter was concerned, the man was too polished. Too refined.

And much too comfortable with his hand on Jessica's back.

Whatever the guy's game, he'd been the perfect date for her, making sure the two of them had hit every cluster of chattering guests, working the crowd with the dedication of a campaigning politician in November. And finally, he'd stopped at Cutter's little band of social renegades, folding Cutter into a knot.

Because, from a distance, Jessica was a knockout—but up close, she was devastating. A red halter-top dress hugged her breasts and narrowed at her waist before flaring gently to the floor. With her hair piled on top of her head, wispy tendrils brushing her graceful neck, her creamy shoulders were exposed in a display that had Cutter's libido beating a drum that made concentration difficult.

She was one-hundred-percent ultra-refined *class*.

Just like the man whose hand clung to the small of her back like an accessory. And suffering through a twenty-minute rundown about Phillip Carr's business was about nineteen minutes and fifty-five seconds more than Cutter could stand.

Phillip was the kind of man any parent would proudly call their son, would go out of their way to claim—despite the fact the man was a pompous jackass. He monopolized the conversation with tales about himself and looked down on everyone in a way that was beyond patronizing. The man sought society's adoration, and no doubt society shoveled it back at him in spades, despite the obvious lack of sincerity beneath the man's intent.

Because the people loved charm, no matter how blatantly false.

And they approved of manners, no matter how bogus the intent beneath the etiquette.

Cutter didn't play those games anymore. He'd bent over backwards to behave as a kid, but it hadn't worked out for him then, and he sure as hell wasn't going to start again now. Suffering in silence was the best he could do. Unfortunately, there was little to celebrate when Phillip finally steered the topic of conversation away from himself.

"There's a new art exhibit at the gallery this week," the man said.

Jessica's face lit up, the sight punching Cutter in the gut. "I've heard," she said.

Phillip Carr aimed his too-slick smile at Cutter. "Have you seen the display of Picasso's work?"

Since the man was gazing directly at him, silence was no longer an option. And somehow, Cutter knew he was being intentionally singled out. "Nope," Cutter said. "I hate his stuff."

Apparently *hate* was too strong a word, because Jessica's gaze cut to Cutter, her eyes widening in a what-are-you-doing? look. The remainder of the group's chatter died, and Philip Carr's face oozed a tolerance that was annoying. Cutter was apparently a simpleton to be pitied because he didn't appreciate the subtle 'nuances' of fine art.

"His work from the later years can be difficult for some people to grasp," Phillip said.

Cutter took the condescending slap in the face without a flinch, calmly taking a sip of his beer before answering, his gaze leveled at the man. "What's there to grasp about a lady with a nose that protrudes from her cheek?"

A tight smile appeared on Phillip's face. "It's an artistic style referred to as cubism."

"Don't care what you call it," Cutter said with a nonchalant shrug, pausing before he went on. "It's still ugly," he said easily.

By now Phillip Carr's smile was huge, but still nowhere near his eyes, and the visual daggers Jessica was hurtling at Cutter were whistling close by. Pissing contests weren't Cutter's usual style, but Phillip's preening-peacock attitude, not to mention his constant possessive touch on Jessica, were grating.

"Picasso was gifted," Phillip said.

"Picasso was anatomically challenged," Cutter returned.

Jessica cleared her throat and, this time, the knife she hurled could have parted Cutter's hair.

"Yes, well…" Flustered at first, Phillip then sent Cutter a condescending look that elevated annoying to hellaciously irritating. "Driving fast around a circular track is hardly a challenge."

The ignorant description of his sport, and the man's agitated look, brought a smile to Cutter's lips as he took another sip of his beer, eyes on Mr. Tuxedo. "Racing can be difficult for some people to grasp."

Jessica chucked an optical barb that hit Cutter smack in the forehead, but he'd had more than he wanted of the conversation. And he wasn't going to stand here and listen to the two of them discuss their opinion of art.

"If we're done with our little artistic critique session," Cutter said, "I'm going to check out the selection at the buffet."

Frustrated, Jessica watched Cutter head towards a table of appetizers set up between a huge tank of puffer fish and an aquarium with floating Portuguese man-of-war. When Phillip began discussing his business yet *again,* Jessica knew it would be a while before he let up. One eye on Cutter, she murmured an excuse to the group and wove her way through the guests, picked up a plate, and went to stand across from him in the buffet line.

Not wishing to attract attention, she kept her voice low. "What was that all about?"

Looking unconcerned, Cutter continued to study the display of food. "I believe I was discussing Picasso with your date while you were giving a running commentary via your visual claws."

"I was *trying* to get you to play nice."

"I don't do nice."

An exasperated breath escaped her lips. "Can't you at least pretend?"

His gaze lifted, spearing her and halting her movements. "Sunshine, whatever you get from me is guaranteed to be one-hundred-percent genuine."

"Insults and all?"

"Insults and all." His lips twisted in suppressed amusement. "It appears you have a problem with my every conversation today."

Jessica tilted her head with false patience at his mention of the day's Battle of the Sexes debate. "I wasn't about to let you encourage Calamity to share her stories of her sexual exploits at work."

The light of humor in his eyes grew bigger. "I like Calamity."

"Of course you do," she muttered. "She has sex on the brain."

"An admirable quality in a woman."

Lips pressed in a line, Jessica kept her eyes on her task as she began to spoon strawberries onto her plate. Why did she let this man's suggestive comments fluster her? "Just because Calamity Jane said she'd pass on a date with the CEO in favor of the firefighter because he'd know how to 'put out her fire'..." Jessica couldn't prevent the roll of her eyes "...does *not* mean she was the instant winner of tonight's debate."

Serving spoon in hand, Cutter paused to look at her. "Love Potion certainly wasn't the winner," he said dryly. "Claiming she'd prefer the CEO because she likes her men both physically *and* mentally commanding was an insult to firefighters everywhere. It also shows her to be an intellectual snob." The humor returned to his eyes. "I'd much prefer hearing about Calamity's escapades."

Her fingers gripped her plate. "Not acceptable."

Cutter stopped in the middle of reaching for a canapé, lifting his gaze to hers. "Why not?"

She shot him a heated look and leaned in, keeping her voice low. "Because she'll only be too happy to tell you about every one of them."

One corner of his lips almost curled into a grin. "You got a problem with that?"

"Yes," Jessica said. After scanning the surrounding guests and finding none of them interested in the two of them, she rounded the table and came to a stop beside Carter. "I have a very big problem with that," she whispered.

And in a weird way she felt oddly left out of every conversation. She was a modern, successful woman. She knew how to flirt. And she was in touch with her sexual self. So why did the banter between Cutter and Calamity intimidate her so?

Cutter leaned uncomfortably close. "What do you have against a few little stories?"

The heat that infused her face was sure to fry the cold shrimp appetizer, and she struggled to maintain her cool. Deep down, she had the awful suspicion that Calamity's details would throw Jessica's entire sex life into sharp relief—sedate, quiet…

And *boring*.

She pushed the annoying thought aside.

Jessica gripped her plate harder. "Sexual relationships are not for public consumption. They should be kept private." She went on, grappling for the right words. "Sharing the details belittles the intimacy between two people and…" Her voice died as she saw the look on his face. "Why are you smiling?"

He hardly *ever* smiled. Hinted at one, yes. Skirted the edges, absolutely.

But full engagement was rare.

And the one he was sending her now sent her body into a sensual tizzy. "Because my bullshit-o-meter is shooting off the charts again," he said.

The surge of overheated blood to her face went nuclear, and she forced her gaze back to the buffet table with no idea what she was spooning onto her plate. "It is *not* bullshit."

"Sunshine," he said as he stepped closer. His voice was low, rumbling with intent. "I don't know who forgot to send you the memo, but sex does not have to be a mystical meeting of two souls. Sometimes it's just a physical release between two people who have the hots for each other." He hiked a brow and the look of desire in his eyes melted her on the spot, fusing her to the floor. "And there is nothing wrong with that."

While her body fought to unwind the tangle of her seared nerves, he turned and headed for another table of food across the way.

Dignity scrambling for a foothold, she scraped her poise up off the floor and crossed to stand beside Cutter. "Maybe for those of you who haven't evolved beyond a lower species of animal," she whispered fiercely.

Cutter's low rumble of laughter sounded rough from disuse, the delight in his eyes obvious. And the full implication of its meaning hit her squarely between the eyes.

Stunned, she said, "You're doing this on purpose, aren't you?"

"Doing what?" The innocent look on his face was clearly false.

"You *are*." She stared at him, perturbed she'd walked solidly into his trap. "You're shoveling out your chauvinistic twaddle just to get me going."

He pressed his lips together, as if suppressing a grin. "Jessica Wilson on her relationship soapbox is a sight to behold." With that, Cutter strolled in the direction of the dessert display.

Heart still thumping from her passionate speech, she blinked and pulled herself together, watching him examine his options for a sugar injection. Finally, she strode across to stand beside him at the display of chocolaty decadence.

"Sunshine..." he said. His hand paused above a plate as he lifted his eyes to hers. "If you keep following me around, people are gonna think you've got a crush on me."

She bit back a fiery retort and sucked in a breath. "And if I strangle you next to a platter of chocolate truffles, the we're-just-friends theory will be impossible to pull off." Cutter ignored her and went back to filling his plate, and Jessica continued, her voice flat. "Exactly how many of our previous conversations were real and how many were for my benefit only?"

"Not saying," Cutter said. "Women like men who are mysterious." He shot her a look brimming with amusement. "Enigmatic." He stepped closer and leaned in. The proximity of his smoldering green eyes sent her nerves skyrocketing. "Men who know how to put out a woman's fire."

Her body felt as if it was being roasted over an open spit, but she stood her ground. "Some of us are more than walking shells of sexual urges, Mr. Thompson." She managed to keep her tone smooth and confident, but her knees were knocking. So she'd never had a wild fling. So her experiences were with men who treated a woman with care. That did *not* mean she was missing out. "We have higher goals in life than simple physical relief. Like romance. Meaningful, *intelligent* conversation." She sent him a wide-eyed innocent look. "Speaking of which…if you'll excuse me, I'm going to find my date now."

His blood pumping from the stimulating exchange, Cutter watched Jessica glide gracefully away, her slender figure elegant as she tossed him a falsely sweet smile over a delectable shoulder.

Jessica Wilson was so sure her emotions were stronger than her physical needs. That basic concepts such as lust and desire couldn't pollute her lofty goals of spiritual connection and happily ever after. She smiled brightly at Phillip as he handed her a dainty flute of champagne, and then her eyes cut in Cutter's direction, a self-satisfied smirk on her face.

Little Miss Sunshine was certainly pleased with herself. Poise bordering on a sanctimonious smugness that tickled Cutter no end. The Battle of the Sexes had just gotten interesting, smashing his off-limits vow towards women until he figured out his life.

Because sometimes exceptions had to be made. Sometimes challenges were meant to be met. And explored.

Namely, Jessica Wilson.

Cutter's gut revved in anticipation, like the shift of lights at a starting line, going from red to yellow to outright, *hell-yeah* green.

The petite blonde in the beaded cocktail dress looked confident in her answer. "Love Potion Number Nine was right.

Most women choose men who provide intellectual stimula-
tion as well as strength," she said, looking around their female
gathering. The lobby was crowded, and Cutter was standing
one group over, but Jessica knew he was listening in. The
blonde sent everyone a smile. "What good are muscles if a
man lacks intelligence?"

Jessica caught Cutter's eye and lifted a brow in triumph,
and his gaze glimmered with amusement.

Not wanting to be surrounded by five women who were
giving a detailed analysis of every online debate since the
beginning of the competition, Phillip had left to corral a potential client in the corner. From her experience during their
first date, Jessica knew Phillip wouldn't resurface any time
soon.

The tall, black-haired lady sent the blonde a supercilious
smile. "Susan, I've been married and divorced multiple times.
Believe me," she said dryly. "A woman can overlook plenty
if her man knows how to put out her fire."

With murmurs of agreement from the cluster of females,
all in support of Calamity Jane's answer, Jessica's smile froze.
As she struggled for a diplomatically worded comment, she
saw Cutter thread through the guests in her direction. He
looked intent on joining their debate. She opened her mouth
to speak, hoping to cut off any comment he might make, but
as he passed by behind her...his fingers grazed her backside,
bombarding her body with wicked messages.

Hair standing on end, heart frantically pumping molten
lead through her veins, she turned to watch Cutter disappear
through a doorway. It took a full thirty seconds for her to recover from the sensual flyby. Or at least long enough for a
single rational thought:

Just who did he think he was?

Ticked beyond belief, body on fire, she murmured an excuse to the ladies and followed in his path. When she crossed

the threshold into the empty corridor, Cutter appeared to take her arm, eliciting a resurgence of the delicious signals.

"You groped me," Jessica hissed, annoyed at her instant reaction to the skin-on-skin contact. Her voice went ultra-high frequency. "In *public*."

"Yep." Cutter ignored her distress as he steered her down the deserted hallway, away from the crowd. "'Cause I knew you'd track me down."

"Groping is unacceptable." Her feet dragged, slowing their progress. "And I had something to add to the group's conversation."

"Hence my actions," he said, guiding her along. "I was saving you from wasting your time. Obviously those women haven't evolved as high up the evolutionary ladder as you. Probably stuck somewhere between spider monkey and chimpanzee."

Her feet finally stopped protesting his movements, her anger easing as she remembered the black-haired lady's comment. "Her priorities are warped."

The look of mild disgust on his face was amusing. "You people are taking this contest way too seriously," he said. "And maybe her experience has taught her the importance of sex in maintaining a marriage."

The light was dim as they headed down the passageway, but she shot Cutter a sharp look anyway. "Or perhaps her warped priorities led to the demise of all her marriages."

Cutter didn't reply, just pulled her into a vast room at the end of the corridor, and Jessica halted in surprise, the last of her anger fading away. Too bad he was still holding her arm.

"You brought me to the shark tank?" she said.

"It's deserted, so it's a safe place for a conversation. Besides," he lifted a brow, "it seemed fitting after your encounter with the professional divorcée." He released her and stopped at the massive glass wall to watch the creatures glide ominously through the water. Cutter turned and leaned a shoulder against the tank. "Speaking of relationship demises, where is this wonderful ex of yours?"

Disturbed by Cutter's focus on her, Jessica stepped up to the aquarium and kept her eyes on a nurse shark as it slowly passed by, the sinuous undulations mesmerizing. "He got called away on business so he couldn't make it."

"And where is Phillip?"

The tone in his voice left no doubt about Cutter's feelings toward the man. For some reason, Jessica felt the need to defend him. "Phillip is brilliant, charming and a sophisticated conversationalist. And yes," she went on at the look Cutter shot her, "he is a little fixated on his business." She cleared her throat. "Right now he's talking to a potential client."

Cutter sent her a questioning glance. "Does this happen to you regularly?"

She studied him, bewildered. His presence made it difficult to concentrate, but it was the expression on his face that finally lifted the confusion.

"Ahhh," she said, with a small smile. Silly man thought he had her all worked out. "I get it." Amused, she tucked her hands behind the small of her back and leaned against the glass, palms against the tank. "You think my attitude towards sex stems from disappointment in my relationships. That I've been withering away like a piece of neglected fruit on a vine."

"Well, there's sex." He lifted an eyebrow suggestively. "And then there's *sex*."

The promise in his voice, and the memory of his touch, set her body throbbing again, but she simply rolled her eyes. "Thanks for clearing that up."

Cutter reached out and touched a single finger to her arm, sending a shock wave of shivers up Jessica's back. The dim light couldn't disguise the heated look in his green eyes. And there was no amusement on his face, just determination and conviction.

He ran his finger from her elbow to her shoulder, leaving a sizzling trail in its wake. "I can clear it up right now."

Her body launched into a sensual tizzy, her breathing forced. "I'm here with a date."

A date of convenience only, and Phillip knew that. But still…

"So having sex with one guy while out with another is a no-no, huh?"

Her heart was tapping so vehemently, the vibration shook her from the inside out. But appearing confident was paramount. And she *was* confident.

"Of course it is," she said. But the intent in Cutter's eyes—and the potential hanging between them—tinted her words with desperation. "And great sex does not take the place of common interests." Lovely, now she was beginning to sound like a ridiculous prude, but everything about the man left her rattled. He stepped closer, enveloping her senses, and her body wound impossibly tighter. Determined to throw him off, she lifted her chin, hoping her voice was calm. "Or scintillating conversation."

Ignoring her lecture, Cutter slowly leaned his head forward, and her nose filled with his musky scent. Sweat dotted the nape of her neck. She closed her eyes, waiting. Anticipating. But instead of kissing her, as she'd expected, he gave her shoulder a small nip.

Desire flooded her every cell, and her palms grew damp against the glass.

The gesture was not meant to be soothing. Or to gently seduce. It held the promise of fantasies her dreams had hinted at but never fully explored. The kind that slipped away when you woke, leaving you wanting, but unsure of exactly *what*.

Lips against her shoulder, he said nonchalantly, "What kind of conversation?"

She swallowed hard, her throat constricted. "Books." He moved to nibble at her ear, and goose bumps pricked, leaving her hair on end again. She bit her lip to prevent a groan from escaping, trying to focus on the cool glass against her hot, slick palms.

What was wrong with her? Where was her backbone? She should push him back. But she couldn't. She should walk away.

But she didn't want to.

Because deep down she wanted to know what those dreams had contained. Intuitively, she knew Cutter could show her.

His mouth moved down her neck, nipping gently, coiling her nerves, searing her skin as he went. "Any other topics allowed?" He pulled her hips against his hard thighs, and her knees went wobbly.

Her mind swimming in the heat of desire, she whispered, "Movies." One of his hands moved higher up her rib cage, and her voice broke a bit. "Good wine, music and current events," she finished desperately, proud she could speak coherently.

He lifted his head to stare at her, his thigh between her legs, and his hand cupping a breast. "Do you want me to do this?" He flicked his thumb across a tip. Her tenuous grip on sanity shattered like crystal on marble, and her nipples went taut, pleasure sluicing down her spine. "Or do you want me to discuss the historical significance of Picasso?"

Staring up at him, she heard her answer come out as an unintelligible mumble. And, as if the babbling words were a signal, his mouth landed on hers. The kiss absolutely lacked gentle finesse. Brimmed with power. Basic. Unapologetic.

Just like the man.

It lit a fire deep within, more decadent than she'd ever known, and kindled her response in return. Jessica reached up and gripped Cutter's shirt, clutching him as her lips met his turn for turn. Hands, large and scalding her through her silk, cupped her backside, and he arched her hips firmly against him, his hard thigh rubbing against her center.

At the shocking skitter of pleasure, a small cry escaped

her, and after several strokes, Cutter pulled his mouth from hers and said, "Maybe you'd rather discuss the merits of imported over domestic wines?"

Her comeback strangled in the back of her throat, desperate for another kiss.

He nibbled on her bottom lip, teasing her as he went on. "Debate the meaning behind the latest foreign film?"

"Oh, for the love of God," she ground out in frustration. "Give it a rest." And like a heat seeker, her mouth sought his.

The kiss went from wild ride to raw need. No hiding behind convention. No subtle hints as to what he wanted. Cutter's grip on her backside grew tight, pulling her hips firmer against his leg, increasing the contact, and twisting her stomach into tight knots of desire. Seconds slipped into minutes as Jessica drowned in the feel of hard lips and harder thigh, a visceral riot of sensation.

Desire wrapped her securely within its grasp, demanding satisfaction. Demanding release. Overwhelmed, she felt tears of pleasure burn the backs of her lids and choke her throat with need. Abandoning her lips, Cutter dropped his mouth to her shoulder again, this time nipping a touch harder, throwing her further into the inferno, and the sharp stab mirrored the ache in her body…and sent her toppling over the edge.

A psychedelic burst of color erupted behind her lids, and her muscles knotted tightly as the pleasure rippled along her body.

Cutter's touch grew gentle as Jessica slowly descended to terra firma. She gradually became aware of the cold glass of the shark tank at her back, Cutter's mouth at her neck, his warm breath on her skin. Her legs felt shaky, and she was definitely feeble in the knees.

Feeble…what an apt description.

After all her stupid, prudish attempts to keep him at arm's length, it only took a single nip to get her to drop her ideals faster than she could scroll past an unsuitable online match.

Cutter straightened up, but Jessica kept her eyes closed and somehow found her voice. "I do not want to see one ounce of smug satisfaction on your face."

His voice managed to convey the emotion anyway. "Agreed." Jessica opened her eyes and met his gaze as he went on. "I'll just say I told you so and leave it at that."

That was because the brash look in his eyes was all he needed.

Jessica, still wobbly and too shell-shocked to engage in further conversation, allowed Cutter to take her arm as he led her back up the empty hallway. As they neared the lobby, she finally managed to move under her own strength.

With a sinful expression on his face, he gazed down at her. "You look like you could use a drink," he said. She'd never seen him so animated before. "Why don't you hunt your sparkling conversationalist of a date down, and I'll tell the waiter to bring you more champagne."

She narrowed her eyes at him and repressed the utterly unfamiliar and completely undignified urge to stick out her tongue. They passed into the lobby, and, after tossing her his signature almost-grin, Cutter turned in the direction of the bar.

From seemingly nowhere a reporter from the *Miami Insider* materialized in front of him, and an irritated expression, mixed with resigned acceptance, crawled up Cutter's face.

"Good to see you again, Mr. Thompson," the reporter said. The bad toupee and snarky smile didn't look any better teamed with a tuxedo. "The sporting world was beginning to think you'd avoid the press forever."

Cutter's face closed down, all pretense of patience gone. "I've been working on a project."

Undaunted by Cutter's attitude, the journalist's smile grew bigger. "Just one question."

Cutter's green eyes went to granite, and Jessica held her breath as the reporter went on.

"Why did you bump Chester?" the reporter said.

Cutter frowned, his tone dismissive. "It doesn't matter. He won and I didn't."

Hoping that was the end of it, Jessica blew out her breath. But when Cutter tried to continue into the lobby, the reporter stepped in front of him, blocking his path.

"But Chester had been pushing the lines of fair play, and most of the drivers were calling for ASCAR to step in." The journalist shot Cutter a meaningful look. "There was a lot of bad blood building between you two." The reporter paused, but when Cutter refused to reply the man continued. "Some say it was your competitive nature going for the win. Some say you took one for the team to teach Chester the rules of the track." The pushy newsman cocked his head. "So why did you take the risk?"

A scowl now permeating his every pore, Cutter stepped around the man. "At this point, the reason is irrelevant."

The reporter watched Cutter get about ten feet away before calling after him, the words sinking Jessica's heart. "It is when it turns ASCAR's number-one driver into its biggest has-been."

CHAPTER FIVE

HAS-BEEN.

Washed up.

Springsteen's voice wailed in the garage. Hips pressed against the 'Cuda as he leaned forward under the yawning hood, Cutter wrestled with the bolt on the air filter. It didn't need changing as much as he needed something to keep him from pummeling the car in anger.

Used to be he would have taken out his feelings with a practice run around the track. It was zooming two hundred miles an hour in his car that had gotten him in the zone. Made him feel alive and eased all the black emotion.

But that wasn't an option anymore. Ever since he'd screwed up his life, he felt as if he'd been bound and gagged. And with the release valve of racing now gone, the pressure of negativity was building in his chest, making him downright surly.

Not that he'd ever done cheerful.

After he'd left the aquarium Saturday night, he'd spent Sunday beneath the car. His ribs still sent crippling reminders of the grueling twelve hours of overexertion. The two-hour exercise binge this morning hadn't helped either. By his tenth set of bench presses, his shirt was stuck to his damp skin, and his chest screamed in protest. In a way, the constant agony was a relief, keeping his thoughts from drifting back to the reporter's question. Still, Cutter knew it was going to be a major ibuprofen, ice-pack kinda day.

Struggling with the bolt, irritated at the filter's stubborn insistence to remain locked in place, Cutter tossed a cuss word at it, just for good measure.

Tally so far? 'Cuda one, Cutter zilch.

"Maybe you should try sweet-talking it," a voice called from behind him.

Jessica.

After a brief pause, he gripped the wrench tighter. "I don't do sweet," he said as he continued his tussle.

And he was in no mood to chat with the beautiful lady. The pain in his chest mirrored the chaos churning in his mind, and neither was leaving him in a sociably acceptable mood.

Or more accurately, his mood was even less social than usual.

"I'm not going away just because you're ignoring me," she said.

The sound of heels tapping was followed by the death of a guitar on the stereo, and the resulting silence vibrated in the air like a washing machine set on spin.

Her voice came from behind and was soft, yet stubborn. "Burying your head beneath that car is not going to fix your problems."

The lady didn't know the half of it, and Cutter just managed to suppress the scowl. "Didn't say it would."

"That's the problem," she said. "You're not saying anything at all."

Jessica leaned on the front of the car next to him, her spicy scent invading his senses, turning him on, revving him up. His emotions. His lust. Even the bitterness. But it was the memory of her beautiful face as she came that swamped him the most.

Cutter raked a frustrated hand through his hair. He didn't need a damn do-gooder coming around trying to do-good on him. What he needed right now was to be left alone. And if Miss Sensitivity couldn't pick up on that, he might as well go take that shower he *should* have taken after he pumped iron this morning. Might ease the pain knifing him in his ribs.

After straightening up, he tossed the wrench at the tool box, and it landed with a loud clatter. "Talking doesn't change a thing."

"You don't know that until you try."

He stared at her lovely face. The wide, expressive brown eyes looked at him with uncertainty—wariness mixed with a generous dollop of fear. No need to wonder *why*.

After the aquarium episode, she clearly didn't trust herself around him. The speed with which she'd come apart in his hands had been stunning. And if it had shocked the hell out of him, there was no guessing the size of the jolt she was recovering from.

The thought brought a large measure of satisfaction that almost chased away his foul mood, but the compassion in her face brought it all back. Her sundress exposed the creamy skin of her shoulders, and her long, leggy look ended in a pair of flat sandals. Feminine. A girly girl. A lady who loved to roll out a spotlight and shine it on every feeling. Analyze it from every angle.

"Sunshine," he said, his voice deceptively quiet as he stepped closer. Her lids flared briefly, as if unsure what he'd do next. Good, she should be nervous. "If you're smart, you'll scram." He shot her a look he *hoped* would end their conversation and headed towards the door. "I'm going to take a shower."

Absently gnawing on the inside of her cheek, Jessica watched Cutter disappear inside the house. Why was she even here? She should definitely go. But when the reporter had called him a has-been, the look on Cutter's face had stolen her breath. And it was that expression she kept seeing. That and the one of smug satisfaction after he'd brought her to her figurative knees…while she was out on a date with another man.

The memory rolled in her belly. Granted, the only reason Phillip had agreed to go to the affair was to push his business at the function. But still, her part in the incident left her slightly queasy. When Cutter requested help with his flirting responsibilities, she'd called him unromantic and unethical, but what did her actions make her?

She closed her eyes and pinched the bridge of her nose. Probably best not to answer that question. But just as divorce didn't preclude her belief in forever, one little indiscretion…

Jessica's mind drifted back to the monumentally sensual moment by the shark tank, a shiver coursing up her spine.

Okay, so *little* was a gross understatement. But one brief moment of weakness…

The excuse died, cut off by the memory of her clutching Cutter, desperate to bring his mouth back to hers, prolonging their contact and drawing it out, until she practically demanded he finish the job.

Okay, so it hadn't been brief either.

With a grimace, she racked her brain, searching for a better platitude.

Ah yes, the oldie but goodie: We learn from our mistakes and move on. That one worked nicely. Thank God for rationalization.

With a small breath, Jessica rubbed her forehead, staring at the closed door Cutter had disappeared through. Instinct told her to go, to leave him to his brooding. But the only reason he'd gone to the party, and had hence been waylaid by the reporter, was to help her with her publicity problem.

With a forced exhalation, she crossed the garage and went up the flight of stairs to the living area. Down the hall a door was open, and she heard a cabinet door close and water running. Her belly exchanged nausea for anxiety as she slowly approached the doorway and leaned against the frame.

The bathroom was done in gray marble dotted with gold fixtures. Glass blocks enclosed the shower, water spraying from the showerhead and steaming up the enclosure. Cutter stood at the double sink, hands on the hem of his T-shirt, as if about to take it off.

Their eyes collided in the mirror, locked, and—for a brief moment—the intimacy of their surroundings almost chased her away. The dark expression on his face hardly helped. But she persevered.

"Even Cro-Magnon man, limited though his vocabulary was, probably expressed a feeling or two when he was upset," she said.

He dropped his hands to his sides, and his gaze slid to the sink. "I'm not upset."

She slowly entered the room. "I'm not leaving until you talk to me."

"Why?"

"Maybe I feel responsible for dragging you to the function in the first place."

His gaze crashed into hers again. "Consider the shark tank payment in return."

A burning sensation hit her between the legs and in the face, all at the same time, though they had vastly different meanings. Ignoring his suggestion, she went on. "So what's bothering you?" Jessica studied him in the mirror. "The loss of a career, the injury…or is it the loss of the adoration of a tabloid journalist with a bad toupee?"

His scoff was one part disgust and two parts skeptical amusement. "I don't give a rat's ass about the press and their opinion." Cutter leaned forward and braced his arms against the counter. "And yeah, I'm ticked my racing career is over." There was a tiny lift to his eyebrows. "Not all of us can be optimists."

"Are you making fun of me?"

He looked at her dryly. "I'm stating facts."

True. It was all she knew how to be. After a period of mourning over her parents' divorce, she'd looked for the positive, grateful their split had been amicable. After grieving over the death of her marriage, with Steve's help she'd dusted herself off and redefined herself.

What other choice had she had?

She tipped her head curiously. "Why did you let the reporter's questions upset you?"

After a quick pivot, Cutter opened the shower door and cut off the water. He turned and leaned back against the glass blocks, hooking his thumbs through the belt loops of his jeans. His T-shirt clung to his every muscle, his ankles crossed. The stance was casual. Easy. His life might be in turmoil, but he was at home and sure of his physical presence. He was the epitome of masculine beauty.

But his eyes were directed somewhere beyond her, his gaze distant. And when he finally spoke, the words surprised her. "I have no memory of the wreck."

She stared at him, the last droplets of water dripping to the shower floor as she processed the news. But, given an option, who would choose to remember such a frightening ordeal? "That's probably a good thing."

"Is it?" he said, slowly shaking his head. He still refused to look her in the eyes. "One minute I was in the lead and the next I woke up in agony, my left hand weak." The muscles in his jaw tensed. "And I knew my racing days were over." It was clear from his tone that the realization had been worse than the physical pain. His expression was hard, though his voice was soft as he went on. "I made a decision that ended it all, and I can't even remember why."

She studied him for a moment. "It would be tough to lose a career."

"It was more than that." He swiped his hand through his hair, as if frustrated, and then crossed his arms, finally meeting her gaze. "Since I was a teen, I've never been a laid-back kind of guy. I don't go along to get along. I don't smile if I don't feel like it. And the track…" He gave a faint shrug, as if searching for the right words. "The track was the one place where I could be myself."

After a brief pause, she lifted an eyebrow wryly. "Disagreeable?"

Instantly, his lips twisted in a repressed smile. "More like I didn't have to pretend to be agreeable." The seconds ticked by as she turned his words over in her head. It was impossible to picture Cutter going out of his way to be pleasant. "Racing suited me," he said simply, and a shadow crossed his face. "And now it's gone."

Gone.

The short word was long in meaning, and it struck a chord in Jessica. This was something she could relate to. The end of her marriage wasn't quite the same, but there were definite similarities. Been there, felt that.

Jessica went to stand beside him, leaning a hip against the counter. "Cutter, I know what it's like to feel lost."

His voice sounded unconvinced. "You're comparing my injury to your divorce?"

She folded her arms in front of her chest. "I know you think marriage is a bunch of bunk, but it was the loss of *my* dream." His brows scrunched together with doubt. "And regardless of whether you agree with my choices, I still had to pick myself up and move on," she said. The sarcasm on his face eased a touch, and he took on a more thoughtful look, as if considering her words. Encouraged, she pressed on. "And you'll only find your way again by taking active steps. Which isn't possible if you're hiding from the world by burying yourself beneath your car."

"Right now all I have is the 'Cuda. When that's done, what do you suggest? I find another career? Racing is all I've ever known. It's all I've ever done. It's all I've ever *wanted* to do."

"You find something else you love, too."

"I don't love anything else."

"Then you find something you love almost as much. But if all you do is concentrate on what you've lost, you'll never be able to see what you have left. And Cutter," she said, taking a small step closer, "your negative attitude is blinding you from the possibilities."

He looked at her as if she was nothing short of crazy. "What possibilities?"

She brushed her hair from her face in exasperation. "I don't know," she said, dropping her hand to her side. "Only you can figure it out." She took another step forward, holding his gaze with hers, enunciating each word for emphasis. "But that won't happen until you *stop* feeling sorry for yourself."

Cutter stared down at her face for what felt like two eternities, and then some. Finally, his lips twitched again, losing a little of their edge. The hard set to his face softened with a hint of humor. And the light in his eyes was a definite improvement over the bitter skepticism. "No one likes a whiner, huh?" he said.

Amazed by the transformation, a smile slipped up her face before she could stop it. "No."

The cereal-box trademark suggestion of a grin infiltrated his face, sending electrical signals tingling along her nerves. When he took a small—but very meaningful—step in her direction, the tension in the air shifted, taking on definite sensual undertones.

After swallowing hard, she pushed away from the counter. "I'll leave you to your shower."

"Wait," he said, reaching into a drawer and pulling out scissors. "Right before you appeared to dispense a dose of that sassy sympathy of yours…" The light in his eyes grew bigger, as if still amused by her accusation of self-pity. He certainly didn't look offended. "I tried to take off my shirt and discovered how bad a number I did on my ribs during my workout. I can't lift my arms without experiencing all kinds of pain." He held out the scissors, the teasing expression back in full force. "Cut my shirt off for me?"

Heart tapping in her chest, she frowned at the obvious setup. She glanced at the ASCAR T-shirt covering his chest. "You'll ruin it."

"Sunshine, I've got a million of them." His brow crinkled in amusement. "What about a little compassion for a man in pain?"

Jessica narrowed her eyes. "You know," she said, swiping the scissors and pointing them at Cutter. "You deserve it for continuing to push yourself before you're fully healed." Eyes fixed on her task, she began to snip from the hem towards the neck, the stretchy cotton parting to display a flat stomach and nicely defined pectorals. The vision was more disturbing than she'd prepared for, than she could *ever* prepare for, her fingers growing clumsy as his chest was revealed. The mix of musky cologne tinged with motor oil was mesmerizing. She stepped back, the shirt now completely split, the sleeves clinging to his shoulders.

Nothing moved but his eyebrow. "I still can't shower."

The fun wasn't over yet. After heaving a large sigh, she said, "Turn around."

Cutter presented her with a back large enough to require a GPS to find her way from one side to the other. But it couldn't be nearly as disturbing as the front. She cut up the fabric, exposing a beautiful expanse of corded muscle, sinew and tanned skin. Who'd have guessed his back would be as impressive as his chest?

Stunned, Jessica gripped the scissors as Cutter turned around. Chest. Back. Gorgeous. Or breathtaking. Either view, Cutter Thompson was eye candy of the sweetest kind. Sure to rot every thought in even the most rational of brains.

And she *used* to excel at being rational.

He cleared his throat, startling her into taking action, and she jerked both sleeves down his arms.

Cutter grimaced with a small hiss. His pain had clearly been real. "Nice touch," he said through clenched teeth. "Your seduction efforts would have worked if it wasn't for the agony."

"I am *not* going to seduce you."

"No return favors, huh?"

Her cheeks burned with memory. It grew worse when Cutter, his hot green gaze fixed on hers, pulled the snap on his jeans, exposing a little more of his flat abdomen. Her heart started banging harder beneath her ribs, sending her messages, as if the rest of her body was too stupid to notice the danger.

His mouth hinted at a smile. "Sure I can't change your mind about that, too?"

Too. As in *also*. Just like he'd proven her wrong by the shark tank.

Without a word, Jessica turned and forced her feet down the hall, trying to ignore the sound of his jeans hitting the floor and the shower door opening. He was back there. Naked. And willing. Water streaming down his beautiful back and buff chest. And after the blatant invitation, all she had to do was strip off her clothes and follow him into the shower.

The mental image left her legs unsteady, and her footsteps faltered.

After rounding the railing, she descended the staircase, her steps growing firmer as she went. Her resolve strengthening with every stride.

She'd already tasted the dark desire he stirred. A bigger slice might choke her focus for sure. Touching him again was out of the question. He was too tempting, encouraging her to stray from the path she'd laid out the day she'd signed her divorce papers. Cutter made her question her vow to stick to her well-thought-out plan for finding a partner.

The *right* partner.

Jessica exited the front door and slipped into her car, gripping the steering wheel. Her heart still thumped shamelessly, and her body, hot, aroused and eagerly pleading its cause, was insisting she take Cutter up on his offer.

But logic was her ally.

Setting—and reaching—her goals was her specialty.

Unfortunately the fundraiser and keeping The Wildcard on a leash and wearing a muzzle had sidetracked her. Cutter Thompson wasn't the only man on the planet with sex appeal. It was time to start searching again. If she looked hard enough, she knew she could find a modern guy who not only wanted a relationship, but connected with her on both a physical *and* emotional level.

A man who knew how to play nice and be polite.

A man who believed in forever, like her.

The curvaceous redhead on the sidewalk clung to the muscle-bound blond as if he required an anchor to keep him grounded on earth. The two were smiling at each other, one set of perfect white teeth flashing, and another set answering the call. Frowning, Cutter watched the love-fest from his low-slung sports car parked in front of the office plaza that was home to Perfect Pair.

Jessica, as graceful and beautiful as ever, stood talking to the couple at the front door. Her tailored skirt ended above the knee, accentuating her long legs. Her cranberry-colored blouse made her olive complexion glow. The dark, glossy hair was partially pulled back, hanging in gentle waves to her shoulders, exposing the arch of her neck and framing her smiling face. The happy couple obviously brought her immense satisfaction.

Cutter studied her, captivated by her expression.

Her unyielding enthusiasm—her steadfast optimism about love, relationships and the potential for the future—

was intriguing. She could have taken her ex-husband for all she could get and spent the rest of her life pleasing herself. Shopping and doing lunch with friends. Bitterly complaining about her ex's faults, her crushed dreams and life's little cruelties.

Instead, she'd chosen to spend her days helping other divorced people find love. Now that he knew her better, it was hard to take her breakup cavalierly. And while he didn't buy into her belief of happily ever after, it was clear the woman had taken her lumps with dignity and turned her misfortune into something positive.

Unlike him…a man who'd been knocked on his ass by a catastrophe of his own making, unable to figure out how to get back up. And if he was completely honest, Jessica was right. He was still throwing himself a massive pity party.

And nobody likes a whiner.

The memory brought a faint smile to his lips. Maybe it was time to borrow a page from Jessica's book on self-improvement and pull his sorry self up by his bootstraps and start moving on.

Satisfied by the decision, when the couple on the sidewalk left, Cutter exited his car.

He knew the moment Jessica spied him, her body growing tense, a guarded look in her eyes. But her caution didn't prevent her usual gracious manners.

"Thanks for agreeing to stop by here," she said as he came closer. They entered the building, and she paused to lock the front door behind them. "I'm meeting someone for dinner on this side of town in about an hour."

He found her news…disturbing. Hit with her delicate scent, and a sharp twist of the ever-present desire, Cutter stepped closer. And had the satisfaction of seeing her eyes grow more uneasy in response.

Good. She still felt it, too. She might be eating dinner with another man, but there was no way she could deny their burning attraction. Several days after their encounter at the aquarium—and the snapping tension in his bathroom—his body's reaction was triggered just by her presence. Desire had become a living, chest-heaving entity.

And it was only a matter of time before Jessica Wilson gave in.

"A date, huh?" He struggled to maintain a serious face. "Firefighter or CEO?"

She shot him a dry look. "Neither," she said as she turned and headed down the hallway. "He's a pharmacist."

Cutter pursed his lips and fell into step beside her. "Unless he's packing Viagra, it'll be hard to put out those fires wielding nothing but a bottle of pills."

She kept her eyes straight ahead. "He's only thirty. I doubt Viagra is necessary."

"You never know," he said. "And are you sure he believes in forever?"

"He's already made the commitment once."

"I smell an oxymoron coming on."

She sent him a cutting, sideways glance. "He and his wife divorced two years ago."

"Am I the only one who sees the irony in this?" When she didn't meet his gaze, he went on, trying a different tactic. "He might still be stuck on his ex."

She halted in the doorway to her office and leaned her back against the doorjamb, arms folded, a familiar look of forbearance on her face. "Mike and I have a lot in common. We're both professionals who enjoy helping people. We have a shared interest in jazz music. And we're both looking for a long-term relationship." Jessica held his gaze, as if everything she'd said was aimed directly at him. "But the main reason I agreed to meet him is because we connected over an in-depth email discussion about divorce."

"That's romantic." He leaned against the opposite side of

the doorjamb. "What happened to the number-one rule of being positive?"

Was it his imagination or was she clenching her teeth?

"When two people click," she said evenly. "The rest is frosting. And romance is more than candied hearts, roses and candlelight."

"So comparing divorce settlements is the twenty-first-century thing now?" he said. She lifted her eyes toward the ceiling in that heaven-help-me way of hers he never grew tired of, and a grin threatened to overtake Cutter's face as he headed into her office. "I suppose we'd better get started. Wouldn't want to keep Mike and his bottle of Viagra waiting."

An hour later, Cutter leaned over the back of Jessica's chair and stared at her computer screen, the last response blinking on the monitor.

Complete honesty should always be a priority.

"Damn." Cutter frowned. "Thank God that's over. It was like trying to flirt with someone's straitlaced grandmother." His frown grew deeper. "I hope Too Hot to Handle doesn't get voted to be my date."

Jessica shot him an amused look. "She's not that bad."

"So if she asks me if I like her dress, and I hate it, she wants me to tell her the truth?"

"There is always a way to phrase things diplomatically."

"Sunshine," he said dryly. "There is no diplomacy in ugly." He rested one hip on her desk and hooked his thumbs through the belt loops of his jeans, looking down at her from his perch. Her scent was driving him crazy as he tried to identify the fragrance. "You seem to have hit it off with her. Maybe the two of you should attend the benefit dinner together. When Calamity Jane wins me as her prize, we could double date."

"I'll find my own date, thank you very much." Jessica

leaned back in her chair. "And Too Hot is only trailing Calamity by four percent. After our first airing went viral on the internet, people are now tuning in from all over the country, making this the number-one most anticipated pairing since the last episode of *The Bachelor*." Jessica's smile was radiant, her bottomless brown eyes bright with delight. It took every ounce of self-control he possessed to keep from pulling her into his arms, much less listen as she went on. "The Foundation has grossed one million dollars on the voting alone."

At the astronomical number, both his eyebrows lifted in surprise before settling into a position of doubt. "I'm not sure if I'm encouraged by the generous nature of our fellow countrymen or disturbed by their questionable tastes in entertainment."

Jessica chuckled. "Careful, Cutter. Your cynicism is showing again."

Enjoying the sound of her laugh, Cutter's lips twisted as he attempted to contain the grin. He failed miserably, and a moment of mutual amusement passed between them. When it was gone, it left the two of them staring at each other.

And the look was full of all those moments he'd wanted her, of her wanting *him*…and more.

The tense silence dragged until Jessica cleared her throat. With a glance at her watch, she pushed back her chair and stood. "If I don't leave now I'll be late."

Late for her dinner date.

Perched on her desk, he gazed at Jessica, studying her intently. Rich, dark hair. Wide exotic eyes. The gentle curves of her breast outlined in her blouse. The low thrum in his body, always present when he was around her, began to thrum harder. If it was time to stop hiding from the world beneath the 'Cuda, it was time to meet their attraction head-on as well. No more innuendo.

"Why don't you pass on meeting Mike and do what you *really* want," he said.

"Which is…?" She stared at him, as if afraid to hear the answer.

"Spend the night in my bed."

Fire spread up Jessica's neck and touched her cheeks, leaving her damp at the nape of her neck. There was no tease in his tone. His sea-green eyes were bright, hard and glittered with a frank desire that sapped the air from her lungs. And as Cutter stared at her, T-shirt hugging the muscles of his chest, his lovely biceps exposed—*God,* she loved those arms—she gripped the back of her chair, steadying her knees as another awkward silence stretched between them.

When she felt strong enough, she opened her desk drawer and pulled out her purse. "I don't have time for this."

Cutter's look of sardonic amusement was absolute and complete. "I love it," he said, crossing his arms across his chest. "You ladies are a piece of work. Honesty is only vital when it's convenient." She bit back the denial as he went on. "When I was in a crappy mood and wanted you to leave me alone, you chased me down and refused to leave until we talked about my *feelings*." He raised a brow at her, the cynicism rolling off him in waves. "But when sex is the subject, you scuttle away and avoid the truth like the plague."

"That's not true."

Okay, so it was. But she wasn't going to admit it.

"Bullshit," he said. "Even after the aquarium, you're still tiptoeing around the two of us."

It took her two tries to swallow against her tight throat. "I'm not tiptoeing."

And that wasn't a lie. She wasn't tiptoeing. She was in all-out commando-crawling stealth mode. Trying to stay beneath the volley of sensual fire raging around her.

The knowing look he shot her left her heart throbbing in her throat. "What a crock," he said.

She didn't owe him anything. One ultra-hot, shark-infested moment in the dark—desire flared high in her body, but she ignored it—did not mean he had some sort of power over her. At least not any she was going to admit to. But she *did* have something to say.

"Okay, here is some honesty for you." She lifted her chin. "I want you to stop coming on to me."

"Why?" He leaned closer. His musky scent teased her, and his green eyes went dark as his voice turned husky. "Because you don't trust the spark between us?"

Yes.

"No. The right guy is more important than any spark," she said. She rubbed her temple, her mind spinning as the look on his face slayed her again. "And because it's making our work on this competition uncomfortable."

His brow crinkled in suppressed amusement. "I must have been gone the day they passed out the manual on when honesty is allowed and when it's not. Apparently it's all about your comfort levels."

Oh yes, indeed it was.

Heart pumping harder in her throat, Jessica forced herself to hold his gaze, twining her fingers through the strap of her purse. "If I don't leave now I'll be late." She didn't care that it was an obvious retreat. She needed time to regroup. "Where shall we meet for the next session tomorrow? Do you want to come by here? Or shall I swing by your place?"

Or perhaps they could engage in a video conference with Cutter on the next continent over. She stared at the handsome cut of his face and the athlete's well-honed body. Make that *two* continents over.

Antarctica should do.

Cutter studied her, as if considering his options for the meeting place. "Neither. I'm giving the 'Cuda a day off." His lips hinted at a smile. "Meet me at my boat at five."

CHAPTER SIX

"Subtlety really isn't your forte," Jessica called out to Cutter.

She watched him emerge from the water in swim trunks, bare-chested and dripping, the Atlantic extending forever behind him. Lining the shoreline were pockets of muted aquamarine and bright turquoise, while in the distance dwelled shades of deep indigo. Sunday Key, a tiny speck of an island, lay just south of South Beach, accessible only by boat. Close enough for cell phone service, but far from rogue reporters.

In shorts and a tank top, Jessica wrapped her arms around her knees and curled her toes into the warm sand. Not that she needed the extra heat.

Because the almost-grin on Cutter's face was more devastating than a tsunami.

Cutter dropped onto the towel beside her and reclined—extending his long, muscular legs peppered with dark hair—and closed his lids.

How could being wet make him look hotter?

His eyes remained closed. "You didn't like today's question?"

"You posted it when you went to unload our stuff from the boat, just so I wouldn't see it." Jessica stared down at him. The responses from the contestants had come in thick and fast, and they didn't bode well for her cause. "And it's a blatant attempt to use your contestants against me."

"I thought you'd be happy I was finally getting into the spirit of the competition."

"Which is more important, the spark or the man?" she said, repeating his posted question to the participants. She narrowed her eyes, frustrated his lids were closed and he was unaware of her glare. "Why don't you simply say I should toss out my priorities and indulge in a succession of meaningless sexual encounters?"

"That's your interpretation?"

Fortunately, his eyes were still shut, so he couldn't see the heat rushing to her cheeks.

Lovely. She'd probably just fallen into some devious trap he'd spent all night formulating. Doing her best to ignore a near-naked—and dripping-wet—Cutter was hard enough, but did he have to smell good, too? No cologne, just a hint of fresh soap, salt water and the vague scent of warm man that Cutter exuded. Maybe it was the smell of testosterone. Or pheromones. God knows he had plenty to spare. And how could she focus on the conversation with him exuding a masculine, lusty cloud that blocked every hope of a rational thought?

Despite everything, talking Cutter into participating in the publicity stunt had turned out better than she'd ever imagined. If she could just keep her physical responses under control, everything would be fine.

A breeze blew the fronds of a palm tree, shifting shadows across Cutter's face. "So how was the Viagra-totin' Mike?" One lid cracked open as he peered up at her. "Prince Charming material?"

The memory of last night swooped in on her, and defeat tried to rise like the undead. Jessica flopped back, stretching out beside him and staring up at the blue sky. Why did her every date seem destined for disaster lately? "More like the Prince of Darkness."

"The Ozzy Osbourne, bite-off-the-heads-of-bats kind?"

"No. A depressing the-end-of-the-world-is-near and I-can't-wait-for-it-to-happen kind."

"Not a happy guy, huh?"

She rolled onto her side and propped her head on her hand, looking across at him, his gaze now fully on hers. "Let's put it this way. He spent the whole evening talking about his ex-wife. And every time he veered off to rehash his breakup—yet again—he started crying." Jessica rubbed her brow with the tips of her fingers. She should have spotted the signs in their earlier emails. "And we're not talking silent sniffles. They were outright sobs that drew the attention of every table around us."

His lips twitched, yet no grin appeared. But there was a definite light in Cutter's sea-green eyes, and Jessica wondered what ocean depth the shade represented.

Certainly nothing deep.

The crinkle of his brow betrayed his amusement. "I could see that coming a mile away." He sent her an innocent look that was so blatantly *not* Cutter it was ridiculous. "At least he was in touch with his feelings."

She flashed him a you're-so-not-funny stab of her eyes. "In touch is good," she said dryly. "Enmeshed is bad."

"Apparently your method for picking your dates is flawed."

If there was one thing she was an expert on, it was dating. She lifted a brow. "I hardly think yours is better."

"You don't even know what it is."

"Sure I do. If you like what you see, you go for it."

As he lay on his towel looking up at her, his expression was patently amused, as if waiting for the punch line. Of course he'd see nothing wrong with his procedure. She, however, refused to be ruled by lust. She'd heard too many stories from her customers about that potentially ugly blunder. She'd made plenty of mistakes on her own, letting her self-centered libido run the show would be worse.

And signing one set of divorce papers was enough—never

again, thank you very much. The murky shadow of sadness peeked from behind her usual positive thoughts, and she shoved it back.

If she stuck to her plan, everything would be fine.

"*You* are reactive." Her tone left no doubt to her meaning. "However *I* am proactive. I don't accept dates with men unless I know we're both on the same page." His eyebrows crept higher, and she could sense his sarcasm coming. She brushed her hair from her cheek. "Ask any online dating service and they'll tell you finding your match is a numbers game. I choose from the database very carefully."

One corner of his lips curled. "Must get tiring kissing all those frogs."

After yesterday, it seemed important to retrace that line in the sand between them. Or, given her previous lapse in good judgment, maybe construct an impossible-to-scale wall. Jessica shook her head. "I don't engage in a physical relationship until *well* after I've established a firm emotional connection."

His look started out puzzled and then landed on disbelief. "You're kidding."

Something in his tone made her defensive. "No. And I don't initiate email conversations until I've ensured a man meets my profile."

After a brief pause—and more disbelief—he said, *"Seriously?"* Cutter rolled onto his side to mirror her position, elbow on his towel, head propped on his hand.

The proximity of those beautiful shoreline eyes was disturbing, and she buried her trembling fingers in the white sand between them, sifting some through her fingers.

His mouth tap-danced around a grin yet never engaged, but his eyes were clearly amused. "Profiling? Isn't that what the FBI uses to track down criminals?"

He certainly seemed entertained by her process. But since

her divorce, she'd honed it until it sparkled like a diamond in the sun.

When she refused to dignify his comment with a response, he finally went on. "So you mean to tell me your *every* relationship begins with the future in mind?" he said. "You never just kick up your heels and enjoy the moment?"

"Cutter…" Giving up on the glares, Jessica tried the feigning-patience route. "I'm not like you. I have emotions. Feelings. Sex is an intimacy that should start with caring. And I don't want to waste my life with men who are inappropriate."

"This is why you're still single. You're too picky."

She lifted her gaze skyward. "I'm *discerning*." She sent him a pointed look. "It's also useful in weeding out the men who are only interested in one thing."

"Sunshine," he said softly. "They're all interested in that one thing."

Heat filled her belly and rubbed between her legs, steaming up her insides, fogging her brain and making it difficult to breathe. If relationships were built on animal attraction, Cutter would be the man for her. But they weren't. And he *wasn't*.

Because sex appeal didn't have staying power, nor was it willing to engage in an intimacy that was a foundation for lasting commitment.

And she would keep rephrasing that reality until her body understood the message.

Unfortunately, the look on his face was almost as mesmerizing as the well-defined muscles of his chest, and she was getting pulled deeper into his gaze. All her good intentions about the need for reality were getting lost in the heat coursing through her veins.

Cutter's phone beeped, breaking the spell, and he reached to pull his cellular from his pants pocket. As Jessica gave her body a stern lecture on the rules, Cutter scanned the screen before glancing up at her. "Too Hot says when two people share a bond, that's all the spark they need." Without a word of discussion, Cutter began to type in his reply.

A waft of concern filled her. "What are you typing?"

He kept his eyes on the screen. "Just my response."

Her anxiety expanded. "Which is?"

A faint lift of his lips appeared, his fingers moving across the keys. "Don't worry. I'm just giving her that honesty she values so highly."

Her frown was instantaneous. "Let me see." Jessica reached for the phone, but he held it just out of her reach. "Cutter." Her voice was sharp now as she wildly sought the phone high in the air. "What are you saying to her?"

The rare sighting of a grin so wide it split his face left her staring in awe, and the sexy rumble of his voice curled her toes. "Just that I hope the kind of bond she's talking about involves whips, chains and handcuffs."

A squeak of dismay escaped her throat. Eyes hurling daggers, Jessica lunged for the phone, and Cutter rolled onto his back with a gravelly chuckle, holding the cellular well out of her reach. His laugh died when she lost her balance and landed with an unladylike thump on his chest.

As she sprawled atop his torso, her heart lodged so high in her throat it blocked all hope for air. Cutter looked up at her, and Jessica's sensory input narrowed to his body beneath her hands, the thud of his heart beneath her palm. The crisp hair. Hard muscle. Hot skin.

The pause was torture. "You know what your problem is?" he said, staring up at her.

Outside of enjoying the cynical man's company?

Or craving his rare smile?

Or the mind-bending, soul-consuming lust that was pumping in her veins this very moment?

Her head swam, and her voice came out as a croak. "What's my problem?"

"You need a guy's perspective while profiling your potential dates."

Jessica gaped at Cutter as she pulsed with an energy that threatened to turn her very existence inside out. A total body inversion. She was fantasizing about the two of them having sex on the beach—and not the alcoholic-drink kind—and he was giving her dating advice?

The impassive face was paired with an amused glint in his eyes. "But this is your lucky day."

Lucky.

The carnal potential to the words didn't bear thinking about.

"How so?" she asked, afraid of his answer.

Another rarely dispensed grin broke on his face. "I've decided to help you choose your next date."

The next day, Cutter parked his car in the driveway of Jessica's quaint, Cape Cod–style home. Immaculately maintained, painted a bright yellow with white shutters, it sported a cozy front porch. The cheerfulness exuding from the house was the perfect reflection of its owner, and Cutter settled back in his seat, amused.

Yesterday, when Jessica had landed on his chest, it had required every scrap of willpower he possessed not to act on the need pounding his body. And it was pretty easy to make out that the feeling was mutual. The rich, hot-chocolaty eyes brimmed with lust. But it was the simultaneous horror in her expression that stopped his raging impulse to roll her over and take what he needed, to give her what he knew she desired.

Because she didn't want to want him.

Staring at the brightly painted, sunny house, Cutter was less than amused now. When he had sex, it was with women who wanted him as much as he did them—no, actually *more*. He'd never pursued a woman in his life. And he wasn't about to start now. The *last* time he'd chased somebody he'd been a seven-year-old kid in hot pursuit as his father had driven away for good. Cutter gripped the gearshift as the unwelcome memory resurfaced.

The day had started out perfect. With his dad's visits growing farther and farther apart, Cutter had been waiting for months to see him. The temperature was warm, the cotton candy was plentiful and the raceway was packed with fans. It was every boy's ultimate fantasy.

Until his father started buying him everything he'd asked for, and Cutter had known something was up. When the race was over, his dad pulled up in front of his mom's house…and finally dropped the bomb. He was moving out of town.

And Cutter had instinctively known he'd never see him again.

Of course, his dad had denied it. And no amount of begging, pleading or tears would change the man's mind. As he watched him drive away, Cutter panicked and took off, chasing the car down the street. And as the taillights disappeared around the corner, Cutter was too winded to keep going.

A car honked somewhere in Jessica's neighborhood, and Cutter's fingers tightened on the gearshift. Damn, he hated that memory. He hated his father for leaving, but he hated himself the most for begging him to stay.

He forced himself to ease his grip and stared at Jessica's door. He was certain they would eventually engage in a hot and heavy affair. But he sure as hell refused to push. He wanted her so ready for him that she hunted him down and demanded he take her. He wanted her actions to be deliberate. Well thought out.

Not an impulsive, spur-of-the-moment decision that would be easy to dismiss as a passing hormonal fluke.

He craved Jessica more than a caffeine addict craved a hit of double espresso at 4:00 a.m. And the spark between them was powerful. Any date she went on now was sure to feel washed-out in comparison to the boiling beaker of chemistry they shared.

So offering some helpful advice about who to meet next in her never-ending line of possible Mr. Rights was a safe course of action. The more time she spent with the soft, touchy-feely, let's-talk-about-our-feelings specimens she chose, the quicker she'd succumb to the sensual vortex pulling them closer.

Pleased with his plan, Cutter climbed out of his car just as a very sleek Italian sports car pulled up to the curb. A black-haired man in a dark suit stepped out, but Cutter ignored him until, a moment later, they were strolling beside each other up the walkway to Jessica's house.

Maybe he was too late to choose her next victim.

"Are you Jessica's date for the evening?" Cutter asked.

The man shot Cutter an assessing look. "I'm her ex." He stuck out a hand but kept on walking. "Steve Brice."

The ex-husband she owed. The one she went out on a limb for.

Nothing about Steve Brice screamed touchy-feely. Business, yes. Sophisticated, most definitely. But certainly not soft.

Cutter warily returned the shake. "Cutter Thompson."

"I recognized you from the paper." Long and lean, Steve cast him a guarded look. "Are you here to take Jess out?" he said, as if sniffing out Cutter's intent.

Why the look? Was he jealous of Jessica dating? Cutter wasn't here to sleep with her—not yet, anyway—and he could take the guy, but he didn't relish the idea of duking it out with Jessica's ex on her front lawn over a misconception.

They climbed, side by side, up the front steps. "I'm here to help her select the perfect next date," Cutter said.

"Yeah?" The laugh from Jessica's ex was neither expected nor malicious. More of a you-have-no-idea-what-you're-in-for kind of chuckle. Jessica opened the door, and Steve's voice dropped to an amused mutter. "Good luck with that."

* * *

Fifteen minutes later, a jazz song played softly in the background, Jessica's laptop rested on the coffee table and Cutter sat on her overstuffed couch, waiting in the living room. The soft colors—muted lavenders and greens—and the presence of enough wicker furniture to fill a Pottery Barn made Cutter feel like a diesel truck in a race with a pretty Mini Cooper.

"I opened a sauvignon blanc if you're interested." Jessica emerged from the kitchen with a bottle of wine and two wineglasses. "Chilled to a perfect fifty degrees."

Steve followed with two bottles of beer, one of them half-empty. "You struck me as more of a beer guy." He held out the full bottle. "I don't know the temperature, but it's cold."

Amused, Cutter gratefully accepted the man's offer. "Cold is good."

Up until now their interactions had been relatively guarded. And when the talk had turned to the new gym Steve's foundation had funded at the local Boys and Girls Club, Cutter had left them in the kitchen to finish their discussion about its grand opening party. Apparently, they were attending it together.

Steve nodded at the photograph of the thirty-year-old Hispanic man displayed on the laptop. "Did you choose the doctor or the lawyer?" He sat on the loveseat across from Cutter.

Jessica took the spot next to Cutter on the couch, and he ignored the instant sense of male satisfaction. "Lawyer," he said. Steve winced, and Cutter bit back the smile. "Environmental law," Cutter added, just to be clear. "He's been a champion for protecting the Everglades. Won the coveted Green Goals award just last year." His lips twitched. "So he's a do-gooder, too."

Steve gave a nod. "Good choice." The man's eyes danced merrily as he sipped his beer. "She does have a soft spot for the altruistic ones."

Like her ex—a man famous for his charitable work. Which

brought up a whole host of questions Cutter had been mulling over since yesterday. Jessica's take-no-prisoners attitude toward dating was impressive, and it led him to assume she was either an over-the-top organizational freak...or she'd been massively mucked about during her marriage.

After meeting Steve, Cutter's curiosity about their married life had grown a thousandfold. Just because the man seemed decent didn't mean he was husband material, but Steve obviously cared about Jessica and wanted to see her happy. So what had done their relationship in?

The thought was cut short when Steve gestured towards the computer. "I told her a long time ago I'd help find the right guy."

Jessica shot her ex a dry look. "There is something inherently wrong with husband number one choosing my dates."

Cutter eyed her over his beer. "Definitely not romantic."

"No." Jessica's gaze cut to him. "It isn't." She paused, and then her face grew curious. "And what do you have against the doctor, anyway?"

"His paragraph stated he'd worked in Angola, Afghanistan, India and Somalia," Cutter said.

She stared at him, as if waiting for more. When he didn't go on, she said, "So he likes to help people, too. What's wrong with that?"

Steve answered for him. "Difficulty focusing."

"Trouble with commitment," Cutter added.

"Probably has a girl in every port," Steve went on.

Jessica poured her wine, picked it up and shifted her gaze between the two men, eyeing them both warily. "Do I get to participate in this discussion at all?"

Despite the fact that Steve had responded too, her gaze settled on Cutter. Another intensely satisfying moment. These two might have been married, they might still be friends, but Jessica's full attention remained on Cutter.

As their gazes remained locked, the tension in the room

stepped up a notch, yesterday's conflict, today's goal—and the delicious potential always stirring between the two of them—all rolled into one. The room vibrated with an energy that should have left the walls shaking.

"You can participate in the final decision," Cutter said. "But if the Prince of Darkness is any indication, I think your track record speaks for itself." As an afterthought, Cutter threw a glance at Steve. "Present company being the exception, of course." After all, the man had saved him from being stuck with a glass of perfectly chilled sauvignon blanc.

Steve raised his beer in a silent salute of thanks, but Jessica kept her eyes on Cutter as she went on with a hint of defiance. "There is nothing wrong with my track record."

Cutter hiked a brow. "Not if you like weepy men."

"Or ones who live in their parents' garage," Steve added.

Amused, Cutter turned toward Steve. "I haven't heard about him."

Jessica's tone was firm. "And you're not going to either."

"He was a doozy," Steve said with a chuckle, which died when Jessica lobbed him a look.

Pink coloring her cheeks, Jessica sipped her wine and then rested the glass on her knee. But she kept her chin high, as if refusing to let her past forays into dating hell get her down. Cutter wondered how she sustained the energy for the constant optimism.

"I still don't understand your problem with the doctor," she said.

Her question had him shifting in his seat to face her as another unwanted memory stirred. He hadn't thought of his dad in years. But lately, long-buried, vague impressions were emerging with a frequency that was disturbing, leaving far-reaching ripples when they surfaced. Even before his old man had left and never looked back, he'd always been changing employers. And every time he'd told Cutter about his new job opportunity, his dad had seemed excited. But none of them had held his attention for long.

And his attention span for his son had lasted all of seven years. Nine if you included the phone calls Cutter received on his eighth and ninth birthdays.

After that, there was only silence.

Trying to ease the tightness in his chest, Cutter threw his arm along the back of the couch, but the twinge of pain refused to ease. "The doctor has been employed by three different agencies and worked in four different countries in less than two years," Cutter said to Jessica. "My take is he's too easily distracted by the shiny objects."

She tipped her head, clearly not following. "Shiny objects?"

Who knew if Jessica's coveted doctor filled the same bill as his father? Their actions—at least on paper—were similar. "No matter where he is," Cutter lifted a brow meaningfully, "or *who* he's with, the lure of possibility is more interesting than the reality in front of him."

He studied the very beautiful, very real woman sitting by his side.

Jessica lowered her brow doubtfully. "The grass is always greener on the other side of the fence?"

"Greener grass. Shiny objects." Cutter hiked a shoulder dismissively. "It all means the same thing."

She lifted her glass and then paused, gaze locked on his, the dark melted-chocolate eyes holding him captive over her wine. She didn't look convinced. Maybe she didn't *want* to be convinced. "You can't possibly know the reasons behind the doctor's actions."

"True." Cutter leaned forward, bringing his head a little closer to hers. "But Sunshine," he said, pleased as the pulse in her neck began to bound faster. "You're gonna have to let him through that grueling prescreening process of yours and actually *meet* the guy to find out."

Jessica's eyes smoldered, but Cutter wasn't sure if she was irritated by his mocking reference to her dating rules…or disturbed by his proximity. He had a feeling it was both. The moment grew longer, the air popping with electricity, until Steve cleared his throat. Cutter turned to face him, realizing he'd forgotten the guy was in the room.

Jessica's ex had a look of intense amusement on his face as he set his beer on the coffee table and stood. "I have a business dinner I need to get to, so I'll leave you two to it," he said. "Jess, don't forget the Boys and Girls Club dinner starts at seven on Saturday." Steve crossed the small space and leaned in to kiss her on the cheek. "Good luck with your plans tonight." And as he straightened up, the look he flashed Cutter was filled with awareness, as if he was onto Cutter's strategy. "You, too."

Steve's smile added a silent '*You're going to need it.*'

CHAPTER SEVEN

As they stood in front of Puerta Sagua restaurant, the scent of tomato and garlic Cuban *sofrito* permeating the night air, Kevin smiled at Jessica. His dimples reappeared for the hundredth time that night. "Would you like to have dinner again this Saturday?"

Jessica stared up at him. The man was perfect. Interesting. Funny. Polite and articulate. And the blond, blue-eyed good looks were certainly nice. She'd been on the receiving end of several jealous looks from their waitress. And yet, throughout dinner, Jessica had compared him to Cutter with every word that came from his mouth.

After all the time she'd spent with Cutter, frustrated by his attitude and the brash words that drove her crazy, she couldn't even get a rest while out on a date. In his absence, her mind had been supplying all the sarcastic observations he *would* have made if he'd been there. Kevin's mention of the art gallery had started it, and the next thing she knew she was filling in for Cutter in his absence—a Wildcard running commentary in her head.

Most distracting.

Frustrated, Jessica smiled tightly as she met Kevin's gaze. "I'll be busy this weekend." Busy figuring out how to get Cutter Thompson out from under her skin. And the desperate hope she'd be successful made her leave the door open for Kevin. "Maybe some other time?"

"I'm looking forward to it."

He leaned in, and Jessica held her breath in anticipation. This was what she'd been waiting for. The moment when all would be redeemed. But when he kissed her oh-so-lightly on the lips, she felt…

Nothing.

No sizzle. No spark.

Not even a weak hint of a faint flicker.

Annoyed with herself, she pulled back and said goodnight—the irritation mounting as she watched him walk to his car at the curb, step inside and take off down the road. And the hope she'd want to see Kevin again took off in the backseat with him.

If a kiss couldn't raise her pulse even a notch above flatline dead, what was the point?

Jessica heaved a sigh and headed for her car parked a little further up the street, ignoring the people streaming around her on the sidewalk.

Cutter had teased her for being too picky in her prescreening process, but this had been the third man she'd met *face-to-face* this week. Each time the evening should have been enjoyable, but it wasn't. Every night she'd gone to bed, listing the favorable qualities of her date in her head, but had slipped into a sleep where her dreams were filled with Cutter. Spine-tingling, erotic dreams that left her shaking with need. Dark, dangerous dreams that left her dying to know how they ended. But she always woke way too soon, heart pounding, her body on fire and feeling unfulfilled.

Awake or asleep, it didn't matter—the man with the rare devilish grin and the cynical attitude was now constantly at her side. Either live and in the gorgeous flesh, or in her thoughts and dreams. At this rate, he would follow her to her grave.

Frowning, Jessica reached her car, unlocked it and slid into the driver's seat, pulling the door closed with a frustration-driven thunk.

It hadn't helped that Cutter had remained silent about her lack of enthusiasm after each date. Amazingly, there had been no sarcastic comments; he'd kept his opinion to himself and helped her choose her next prospect. And damn him, despite his cynicism, he'd chosen well.

In theory, each of the men Cutter had selected looked perfect. But, when presented with the reality, not one of them had clicked for her.

With a sigh, she sank back against her seat and watched the people stroll by on the sidewalk. Tourists and locals. Families and groups of friends out on the town. And then there were the couples...

And why was she enormously successful at helping others find love, but a miserable failure when it came to herself? It was the feedback from her work, the delighted clients who stopped by to thank her, that kept her going. And *hoping*. But lately she'd had moments of worry, times when a small part of her had wondered if Cutter was right about her divorce disqualifying her from her profession.

Lovely, now the man had her doubting her business skills.

But she had abundant proof that—at least professionally—she knew what she was doing. No, her biggest doubts were reserved for herself, because all her relationships had ended in failure. But unlike her female clients, those that had been treated poorly, Jessica couldn't even blame the *men*. Every one of her failed relationships had been with guys that other women dreamed about.

So what did that say about *her*?

Anxiety spread from her gut to her veins, circulating to every corner of her body. She'd held out for the good guys, invested herself and worked hard to keep the romance alive. Yet every single time it had ended, she was left questioning what had happened. Alone and wondering why. The whole it's-not-you-it's-me platitude was getting annoyingly old. It had started with Steve and continued since her divorce.

She had *zero* proof she could be successful at love, so… did that mean she was just destined to fail?

When she was alone, that soul-sucking fear was overwhelming. But now she was so massively attracted to a man who was the polar opposite of what she needed that she couldn't mount a speck of enthusiasm for anyone else. Her body was immersed in a fog of desire that clung to her whether Cutter was with her or not.

She closed her eyes and dropped her forehead to the steering wheel.

Think, Jessica. *Think.* Where is the woman famous for formulating logical plans and following through?

In an effort to cope with the sadness, the day her divorce was finalized she'd mapped out her goals for the future. She'd done it before. She could do it now.

So how did a woman purge a diabolically sexy man from her thoughts? Jessica nibbled on her lip, considering her options. Denying herself hadn't helped. Pretending the attraction didn't exist and trying to move on hadn't worked. And if her body's lack of response to the fabulous Kevin was any indication, she was in serious trouble. So maybe she needed to get Cutter out of her system? Scour away his influence over her by discovering what sex would be like with the bad boy with a bad attitude. End the mystery, once and for all.

The possibility set her heart pumping in a way full-frontal contact with Kevin never could. Maybe it was time to shut off her brain and heart and indulge the body. Just once. She'd never had a one-night stand in her life, had never even wanted one before. Yes, she'd have to deal with Cutter until the contest was over. But she was an intelligent, sophisticated woman. She could handle it.

More importantly, she *had* to handle it.

Because deep down she feared that if she didn't exorcise Cutter from her thoughts, she'd be stuck in this sensual limbo forever. Wanting him for the rest of her life.

Heart thumping like a wild thing, Jessica started her car and pulled out into the street, heading for Cutter's.

Kneeling on the floor of the 'Cuda, Cutter gave the bolt on the driver's seat one more wrench until, satisfied it was secure, he settled onto the passenger bench lining the back of the car, admiring his handiwork.

"Cutter?"

Jessica's voice toppled his thoughts, scattering them. "In here."

Her elbows rested on the door frame as her face appeared in the window. "Why are you sitting here without music?"

"Wasn't in the mood."

The small smile on her face didn't quite reach her eyes, and he wondered why. "Is Springsteen losing his charm?"

"Just preferred silence."

Actually, Cutter had been so busy lately he'd forgotten his need for loud music. He'd installed the carburetor, purchased new tires and today he'd mounted them—leaving his hand weak and his chest throbbing from the heavy lifting. The remainder of his time this week had been spent researching his idea for a new business venture. It was turning out to be more viable than he'd thought. Overall, Cutter was pleased with his progress towards taking back his life.

But not nearly as pleased as he was to see Jessica.

And therein lay the problem.

He studied her for a moment, wondering why she looked distracted. "Your date ended early." No surprise there. If he'd known how safe it was to shove her in the direction of other men, he might have come up with the plan earlier. When she didn't reply, he went on. "What was wrong with Kevin?"

His question brought a slight frown to her lips and she

stared at him a moment more, as if about to protest she'd found anything wrong at all. But she always did. Which, in some ways, he found extraordinarily amusing.

All those do-gooders and not one had captured her interest.

The three successful men had been well-rounded, charmingly funny in their emails and good-looking. One owned several hip hotels that were so cool they'd landed him on the cover of *Entrepreneur* magazine. Hell, Cutter would have dated the man himself—if he'd been oriented in that direction, of course. Which he wasn't.

Jessica opened the car and climbed in to sit beside him, pulling the door shut with a thump and tossing her purse on the seat. Her seductive scent closed in around him. Surprised by her actions, he swept his gaze down and took in the sight. Breasts outlined by her silk blouse, a skirt that ended mid-thigh, offering him an eyeful of bare skin. Yeah, he was definitely firmly oriented in the female direction.

Most notably *this* female.

But why did she look so disturbed?

She stared at the front seat, as though a great secret was embossed in the black leather. With a deep inhalation, she opened her mouth and then paused, biting her lower lip. When she blew out a breath, her words came out in a rush. "I've decided to engage in the first one-night stand of my life."

Comprehension hit him hard, and there was a collective groan of 'about damn time' in his every molecule. The pain in his ribs faded as desire, the living entity that had consumed him for days, throbbed to new heights. He wanted her more than he'd ever wanted a woman in his life.

But the depth of his desire was another snag he hadn't counted on.

And as her words *one-night stand* settled deeper, as if she was already prepared to move on before she'd even experienced what they could share, Cutter frowned—bothered by the limitation she'd set before they'd even started. She'd assumed it wouldn't be good enough to make her want more.

She was writing the whole thing off before the first taste.

Her silky blouse was a brilliant red that made her brown eyes brighter and her skin glow. She looked at him expectantly as his fierce need battled his growing impatience, both with her...and with himself for wanting her so much.

As the seconds ticked by without him responding, she lifted both eyebrows. "Aren't you going to say anything?"

He shifted in his seat to face her. "I'm thinking."

He was pondering how it felt to have this woman change her mind. But not by much. Clearly, he still wanted her more than she wanted him. And he hated being left holding the short end of the stick. Old resentments flared, and it was impossible to ignore that hard-earned childhood lesson.

Never invest yourself in someone who wasn't invested in you.

A furrow appeared between her brows, a faint frown on her lips. "Last week you were trying to convince me to skip out on my date and spend the night in your bed."

The need to needle was strong, and he feigned surprise. "So I'm the lucky recipient of your decision?"

She looked at him as if he were crazy. "Would I come here to tell you I was going against my usual good sense with someone *else?*"

He bit back a bitter laugh at her statement. The woman based her life's work on fostering honest dialogue. And she wasn't sparing his ego now. "Maybe I've decided I don't want to be your consolation prize while you look for something better."

Her frown grew deeper, as if refuting his statement. "It's not about a better man. It's about finding the right one for me."

He lifted a brow dryly. "I hate to break it to you, but your paint-by-numbers approach to selecting a guy won't work."

He considered it a moment more as a new thought washed over him. "Could be the whole reason you're attracted to me is because you consider me unattainable." And the idea wasn't comforting—to be wanted not because of who you were, but because of what you weren't.

"That is not why I find you attractive," she said.

Despite his doubts, the words brought a measure of male satisfaction. But watching her so obviously not wanting to want him was hell. He should teach her a lesson, tell her to go away and come back when she was *really* ready.

But it appeared he'd been damned as a kid and now he was damned as an adult.

Because, even though his ego had taken a hit, he wanted her to stay. Desire was winning the war inside, but he refused to roll over and make it easy for her. If she wanted him enough for *one* night—his gut burned at her limiting assumption—then he'd make her affirm her actions every step of the way.

"Why *do* you find me attractive?" Cutter finally responded.

Staring at Cutter, Jessica's mind scrambled for a response. She'd been asking herself the same question since their first ride on his boat—when she'd wondered what kissing him would be like. And after the soul-wrenching decision to chase him down, to go against every plan she'd laid out the horrible day her divorce was finalized, here he was looking unhappy with her decision.

He'd looked down her shirt during their first Battle of the Sexes session. He'd seduced her beside shark-infested waters and the moment had sizzled in her memories since. So where was *that* guy? The one who had unsnapped his jeans in his bathroom, lust in his eyes, and stepped closer, telling her to let him know when she changed her mind. Well, she finally had, and this was his response?

She bit her lower lip, swimming in a mix of desire and doubt. She'd assumed all she would have to do was tell him,

'Take me, I'm yours,' and he would. But nothing about this encounter was going as expected, leaving her unnerved.

Cutter threw his arm along the back of the seat. "Well?"

Her breaths came faster. "Well what?"

"Aren't you going to seduce me?"

The question knocked her hard, and the jolt to her nervous system probably guaranteed she wouldn't sleep for a month. Jessica gaped at his face. There was no tease in his expression. No subtle smirk that meant he was messing with her. His expression was serious as he waited...and comprehension arrived with a bang.

Oh. My. God. He was going to make *her* do all the work.

Asserting herself sexually within a comfortable, secure relationship was one thing, but in a casual encounter? The kind she'd never had before?

The frank gaze proved too much, and she dropped her attention to her suede skirt, drawing circles in the velvety nap. For the first time in her life she'd made a plan she wasn't sure she could carry out.

His voice was low. "Changing your mind?"

Her finger stalled on her skirt as she looked up. Arms crossed, Cutter was studying her. His musky scent, and the sight of all that masculine beauty, hard and unyielding, stretched her desire tight. And he looked as if he'd wait all night before he'd make the first move.

Her eyes dropped to the gorgeous biceps that fired her imagination with their perfection—powerful without being too bulky. His green eyes glittered with restrained desire, and the cropped brown hair looked as if he'd recently swiped a frustrated hand through it.

All the raw, edgy energy pulsing beneath his surface was evident in his face, driving the heat from her belly to her inner thighs. Time slowed, filled with the sound of their breathing and the smell of his musky soap. Cutter's gaze shifted to her mouth....

And the embers in her gut flared to beads-of-sweat-producing levels.

He'd kissed his first girlfriend in this backseat. Had they made love here as well? But the real question was—did Jessica have the guts to push him to make love to *her*?

Thighs trembling, the mental imagery consumed her and drove Jessica to ignore her doubts. She reached out to lay a palm on his chest, splaying her fingers over hard muscles. Absorbing his heat.

The ever-present glimmer in his eyes intensified. "Sunshine." The words rumbled beneath her hand. "Just be sure this isn't about your frustration that you can't find whatever the hell it is you're looking for."

"It's not."

He hesitated a moment. "And I don't want you turning to me out of sadness either."

She sensed a crack in his resolve. Hope—and the firm chest—made her bolder, and she sent him a faint, teasing smile. "What emotion am I allowed?"

Her thumping heart marked out the passage of time until a trace of return humor touched his face—shortening the leash on her fears and lengthening her need.

His gruff voice skittered up her spine. "Desire is always welcome."

The words tipped the scales heavily in favor of desire. Biting her lip, she considered her options. The delicious sight of denim-covered thighs and a visible erection simplified her decision. She wanted him close. Wiggling her hips, Jessica hiked up her skirt, threw her leg over his lap, and straddled him, her body softening at the feel of steely thighs. Amused by the surprise—and spark—in Cutter's eyes, she said, "That's good to know."

Cutter looked up at her with a laser-like gaze, arms still at his sides, forcing her to continue.

Every cell taut with tension, she tried again, placing both

hands on his chest. She smoothed her palms down his torso, relishing the ripples and longing to unzip his jeans. But right now her fingers were shaky from nerves. Perhaps teasing him would loosen his restraint. "This is your chance to prove to me that great sex is better than discussing common interests."

His eyes smoldered as her hands explored his flat abdomen, but his expression didn't budge. "Didn't I do that already?"

Jessica's limbs grew heavy with the memory, her body burning for his touch. "That was just an appetizer," she said softly, her gaze holding his. Hoping she could *will* him into taking action. "I want the full meal."

His eyes grew dark, going from close-to-the-shore sea green to over-her-head jade, and, desperate for a response, Jessica placed her mouth on his.

The kiss was vastly different from the one at the Aquarium. She'd initiated this one, and she continued to work on persuading the man to join in. A barely there pressure of soft lips against unconvinced firm ones, as if he still wanted more from her, but the feel, the taste and all his coiled energy drove her wild. And any lingering uncertainty began to drop by the wayside. After years of dedication to her well-laid-out plans, after all the worries that had plagued her since her divorce, right now she was sure of only one thing: There was no one she'd rather toss caution aside for than Cutter.

Her breath mingled with his as she teased and tasted her way from one corner of his mouth to the other, coaxing him to participate. His thighs were hard between hers, his chest a solid wall beneath her worshipping hands. And his mouth began to shift slightly, tasting her back. But he didn't touch her.

Dissatisfied with his lack of involvement, outside of his almost reluctant mouth, she ran her tongue along his lip, and Cutter inhaled sharply. With a muttered curse, he finally grasped her arms. But instead of pulling her closer, the way she wanted, he pushed her back several inches, his expression going from restrained desire to serious—and she nearly groaned in frustration.

"I still don't fit your profile, Jessica."

She stared at him, her head swirling with need. She knew what he meant. He didn't believe in happily ever after. He thought true love was a joke. He could make her laugh with a cynical comment, tease her—he'd even sleep with her...but he wouldn't give her a commitment.

Her heart thumped with desire even as her uneasiness grew. But Jessica was tired of holding her breath, waiting for the fascination she had for him to fade.

Most of all, she was tired of wanting this man and not having him.

"All I have to know is—" her finger traced the moisture left by her tongue on his lower lip "—how are you at undoing buttons?"

Eyes on hers, he held her arms as his thumbs stroked her skin, sending electrifying messages. "Slower than I used to be."

Jessica raised her hands to the front of her blouse. "Then I'll undo mine." She started at the top, slipping buttons through the holes. When her bra-enhanced cleavage came into view, Cutter's gaze dropped to her chest, and fire shot between her legs.

"I'll sleep with you." His words throbbed with energy, sapping the moisture from her mouth. "But I won't start boning up on my current events."

Encouraged, fingers still working on her shirt, she bared more skin. "How are you on foreign films?"

His voice grew tight. "I could probably fake a conversation about fine wine."

She finished the last button. "Are you up for Picasso yet?" She slipped her blouse to the floor, her satin bra the only barrier left.

This time his voice was husky, his eyes hungry, but the words were detached. "Picasso was the Paris Hilton of his time. Way overrated."

Jessica had to smile at the man with the blunt words, killer good-looks and well-cut physique. Despite his casual remark, the dark, restless potential surrounded him like an aura, boldly pushing her out of her comfort area. He was a lethally potent mix. Afraid her false courage would fail, she quickly unhooked her bra and dropped it to the floorboard.

"Jessica..." Complete capitulation looked close at hand as his gaze roved every inch of her bared breasts, scorching her skin.

Heart soaring from his look, she basked in the first full drop of what she hoped was the beginnings of enough water to save a woman dying of thirst.

And she was dying for *him*.

Too eager to linger, Jessica slid his shirt up his chest. And though Cutter raised his arms to help, with his back pressed against the seat, removing the fabric was difficult. The tantalizingly limited view of lean abdomen and muscular chest taunted her. Growing impatient, she tugged harder, trying to work the cotton higher.

Arms lifted, T-shirt caught around his shoulders, Cutter infuriated her with the amused light in his eyes. "You in a hurry?"

Her hands paused. "Yes," she said, unable to keep the irritation from her voice. The seduction wasn't going as fast as she'd hoped. "And you could be a little more helpful."

Almost smiling, Cutter leaned forward, finally giving Jessica room to jerk the fabric over his head.

"I should have planned for bigger quarters," she said.

"I figured you'd like the romantic tradition of a backseat."

She tossed his shirt aside, planting her hands on her hips. "Are you ever going to make love to me?"

Without a word, he pulled her close, his mouth landing on

hers with decisive force, giving her a heavenly taste of the hard lips she craved. Raw. Rough. And powerful. His hands kneaded her lower back, fueling her desire, and she melted against him, relieved he'd finally taken over.

His chest hair tickled the sensitized tips of her breasts, and Jessica moaned against his mouth, relishing the feel of the firm muscles she'd battled his shirt for. The moment lingered. Pleasure took a firmer hold. And grew stronger when Cutter's hands abandoned her back for her legs. As he pushed her skirt higher, his thumbs raked her inner thighs, searing her skin, creating an achy longing.

While his hot, wet mouth consumed hers, his thumb reached her underwear-covered clitoris and stroked once, eliciting a jolt of lightning, and Jessica bolted upright, her hands shooting to the ceiling of the car.

Cutter stared up at her, caressing her through the silk. Hands braced against the top of the 'Cuda, she closed her eyes as the agonizing pleasure wound her tighter, her undies growing damp.

His thumb taunted. Teased. Until she was so slick she feared she'd spontaneously combust before they actually had sex. "Cutter," Jessica groaned, lifting her lids to look at him. "I can't wait anymore."

His gazed burned into hers. "Then do something about it." Her stomach swerved lower and her breath caught. His voice rough, he continued. "This is your show."

Her show. Her choice. Her decision. And he was forcing her to confirm it over and over again. So much for Cutter making it easy. But his thumb continued to slay her bit by bit, and she was shaking with the need to be filled by this man.

Willing herself to focus despite the haze of pleasure, Jessica reached into her purse on the seat, pulling out one of the condoms she'd purchased on the way here. Her hands shook with barely contained impatience. And *desire*. Horribly conscious of her trembling fingers, she ripped the package open and the condom fell to Cutter's lap. Jessica stared mutely at the latex lying next to his denim-covered bulge.

A blatant visual of the reality of her decadent, self-indulgent decision.

After a heart-pounding pause, Cutter muttered, "Sunshine, condoms won't work that way."

Despite his measured response, she sensed his need, encouraging her to release his snap and the zipper, her knuckles grazing his hard erection. Cutter shuddered with a small groan, and the reaction was gratifying. Growing more confident, she stroked his shaft, marveling at the soft skin.

The impossibly hard length.

Her wet sex throbbing with urgency, Jessica sheathed him in latex and lifted her hips, aiming his erection between her legs. But as she pulled her panties to the side, Cutter made the final decision for her and arched up.

Plunging deep.

Jessica cried out in relief and dropped her head back, relishing the delicious stretch as, hands gripping her hips, he pulled back and filled her again. And again. Cutter's hard thrusts and languid pace were a blend of sweet ecstasy and delicious torment. Overwhelmed, she closed her eyes and braced her hands on the ceiling again, nails digging into the fabric from the pleasure, praying he'd end the torture soon.

Jaw clenched, Cutter fought to control his breathing, clasping Jessica firmly as he moved beneath her. Their hips rocked with a single intent, straining in unison, the rhythm slow, yet powerful. Purposeful. His need was strong, and though the temptation to take her fast was just as urgent, Cutter held back.

Used to be, patience wouldn't have been an option. But he'd learned the value of it recently. And if one night was all he'd get, he wanted to savor every moment. Bask in every sensation. For the first time in his life, he didn't want to come and go in a rush. And after twelve years of pushing himself to go faster, jockeying for every advantage, reveling in the thrill of barreling at high speeds towards the peak of the ultimate adrenaline rush—both on and off the track—the discovery of the pleasures in a more measured pace was a revelation.

The sight of her lovely body and their undulating hips was too much, and he cupped her breasts, urging her closer for a kiss, slanting his mouth across hers. Her hair framed his face, a silky curtain that smelled of apples and a spice he couldn't identify.

Her softness, sweet fragrance and the satiny feel of her skin contrasted sharply with his hard edges. Despite the contrast they blended well. He was used to being alone, and never had he felt so in sync with another human being. Of all the sexual experiences Cutter had enjoyed, the encounters had never been more than a simple exchange of satisfaction between two people. With Jessica, it was infinitely more, and in some ways that made him uneasy as hell.

Their breathing grew rough, ragged, and Jessica pulled her mouth from his, clutching his shoulders, her exotic eyes dark and desperate. Her whispers urged him on. But even this close to the climax, he was determined to wring every ounce of pleasure from the moment. Instead of increasing his pace, he shifted his hands to the small of her back, increasing the force and intensity of his thrusts. Arching higher. Deepening the contact. Slow, heavy, demanding strokes that pushed the edges of the pending orgasm until it built so high it towered with a frightening promise.

Jessica's nails bit into his shoulders. "Cutter—" Her voice choked on his name.

And he knew. With her shattered look, and her tremble of need, he knew. She felt the massive potential too, and intense satisfaction surged inside him. With every buck of his hips he drove them higher, reminding her that—*yes*—she desired him as much as he desired her.

With every hard thrust, he pushed the ecstasy further, making *sure* she'd never deny it.

Until, both their bodies damp with sweat, Jessica sobbed his name just before she tensed, letting out a shout as she came. The energy pulsed from her muscles to his, toppling his waiting orgasm, pleasure wracking his body.

CHAPTER EIGHT

Two days later the small reception room of Perfect Pairs was crowded, a dozen divorce-group attendees filling the leather couches. It was Jessica's largest turnout since she'd started hosting the meetings five years ago, but her face strained to maintain a smile. When the hour was finally up, instead of lingering over the goodbyes, she retreated into her office, grateful it was done.

Jessica slumped into the chair at her desk, kneading the tension in her temples—every muscle taut since she'd said an awkward goodbye and shot from Cutter's car like the hounds of Hades were hot on her heels.

She should have seen it coming. Until Cutter, all her sexual partners had been involved with her in a committed relationship, and stepping outside that safe domain had been harder than she'd imagined. So when the self-conscious morning after—or, in this case, the moment after—arrived, she'd panicked. Freaked, actually.

And she kept remembering the stunned 'what the hell' look on Cutter's face as she'd fumbled for her blouse before bolting from the car.

Embarrassment hit again. "Oh, God," she groaned, dropping her head to her hands.

She was a confident adult, why had she acted like an awkward fool? Logic and reason were supposed to be her specialties, so why couldn't she have maintained her cool?

Stupid questions, because she knew the answer. Everything about making love to Cutter had come as a surprise. From his initial reluctance to his attitude to the way he'd refused to be hurried. He was a former race-car driver, for God's sake.

So where had been his need for speed? Why hadn't he come and gone in a heated rush?

Deep down, that was what she'd expected when she'd hunted him down. A hard, fast hit of satisfaction. Get in. Get out. And then get *on* with her life.

Instead, he'd taken her with deliberate intent, the intensity overwhelming. Towards the last few deliciously agonizing moments, it was as if he'd sensed her sudden need to hurry it along, to end the torture of feeling so *much*. But he'd purposefully prolonged every little sliver of pleasure until she'd thought she'd die.

And then she had...experiencing the most mind-shattering orgasm of her life.

Memory moved through her, drowning her in desire, and Jessica closed her eyes. She'd never sobbed anyone's name during sex before. Or shouted it out for that matter.

But this time, she'd done both.

"Jessica," a familiar female voice called, and Jessica's heart settled lower in her chest.

Oh, lovely. Fate wasn't done with her tonight. It had shown up to twist the knife and finish her off. Nice.

With another forced smile, Jessica looked up at her office doorway. Susan—a regular support-group attendee after each of her four divorces—was a vivacious, fortysomething brunette who excelled at ending a marriage.

"I came to return this." Susan held out the book *Twelve Steps to Better Intimacy*. "Thanks for loaning it to me."

Jessica rose and rounded her desk, taking the self-help guide. "My pleasure." She slid the hardcover back into her packed bookcase, hoping the woman would sense she was in the midst of a crisis and leave.

But fate twisted the knife harder.

Susan paused, shifting on her feet. As if she had something important to say. "Marrying the men I had affairs with hasn't worked out well." Jessica froze. With a sheepish smile, Susan shrugged. "I guess following the sex wasn't the wisest decision." Jessica's decision to sleep with Cutter made maintaining the calm expression difficult, but she persevered as Susan went on. "But listening to you share your goals has really motivated me to make some changes."

"I didn't do anything," Jessica said. Oh, but she had. She'd glibly assumed she was stronger and smarter than Susan. But is that how people like her got started? One hot, intensity-filled moment at a time? Feeling like a fraud, she said, "I simply suggested a book when you asked for a recommendation."

Susan shook her head. "No, it's your levelheaded dedication to holding out for the right relationship that's inspired me." The irony was so heavy Jessica could barely withstand the weight as Susan continued. "I just wanted you to know I've decided to follow your example."

Jessica bit back the hysterical laughter, hating her new role as a hypocrite as Susan said good-bye. When she left, Jessica sank into her chair.

Where had that levelheaded Jessica gone? She'd been slowly disappearing since Cutter upended her life. Had she really thought sex with him would make things better? Her mind scrambled for a reassuring platitude…but nothing seemed appropriate.

Except maybe the one about hindsight and clarity of vision.

The second she'd returned from orbit and landed back in that car, she'd known Cutter had smashed her plans for exorcising him from her system.

Worse, he was more embedded in her mind than before. The memory of his body seared into hers. And why was the man she'd tossed out her rules for—the one so wholly unsuitable—why was *that* the guy who gave her the greatest pleasure?

For the love of God, he'd had her howling his *name*.

With a growing apprehension, her stomach writhed with nerves. One week and two Battle of the Sexes sessions left to go. And for the first time in her life, Jessica wondered if there was a plan that would save her.

The white paint on Cutter's home reflected the brilliant Florida sun, emphasizing the lines that formed the right angles of the contemporary architecture. Nothing soft. No rounded corners.

Just like the man himself.

After climbing the flight of steps to the second-floor entryway, Jessica glanced anxiously at the doorbell. How long could she stare at the intricate details of the etched glass around the door before he'd find her standing there like a silly coward?

She nervously fingered the strap of her casual halter dress. The bright colors were supposed to inspire confidence, but it wasn't working. When she caught herself staring at the doorbell again, she grunted in disgust and pushed the button.

You can do it, Jessica. Just get the contest done. You don't need a plan beyond that. And just try *to pretend—*

The door opened and Cutter came into view, knocking her pep talk from her head.

She had no idea what he was thinking, the hard planes of his face impassive as he leaned in the doorway, hands hooked on his hips. The snug jeans and black T-shirt left little to the imagination—except she had no need for one now. She had memories scorched so heavily on her brain they'd never be scrubbed away. The waves of brown hair were damp, as if he'd just showered, and he eyed her dryly. "You're back."

His statement, and the look in his green eyes, only served to remind her of how she'd left, and heat slid up her spine. "Of course I am." In an attempt to appear unflustered, she sent him a cool smile. "We have work to do."

"Oh, yeah," he said with a hint of sarcasm. "The Battle of the Sexes."

He stepped aside to let her pass. She felt his gaze on her as her high heels tapped against the hardwood leading to his modern living room. The expansive floor-to-ceiling windows displayed the sparkling Biscayne Bay as if it were a tropical mural painted on the wall. Sunlight streamed inside, glinting off the glass-and-chrome accents in the room. Jessica studied the contemporary furniture, trying to decide where to sit. The leather couch implied intimacy, and she couldn't stand around like a fool forever, so she targeted the mahogany bar in the corner.

Cutter's voice came from behind as he followed. "I thought you were here to finish my promised one-night stand."

Her body flooded with memory, fire pooling between her legs, and she almost tripped on the plush rug. She climbed onto a bar stool, resting her overheated palms on the cold marble as he rounded to the other side. When he braced his hands on the counter, his biceps grew more defined, and her body hummed the familiar tune of desire. She held her tongue as he gazed at her expectantly.

And Jessica fought to remain calm in the face of the world's most perfect male storm.

"Or was the 'Cuda all the night I'm allowed?" he finally went on.

Keen to hear Jessica's reply, Cutter raised an eyebrow wryly and waited. The tense look on her face would have been vaguely amusing if he wasn't so worked up himself.

When she spoke, there was no answer to his question. "May I have a drink?"

He pursed his lips and studied her. Silky brunette hair hung in waves to bare shoulders, and her dark eyes looked troubled. The halter top of her dress clung to the breasts that had haunted his dreams since the 'Cuda, and lust returned with a vengeance to his veins.

He could definitely use a drink.

"All I have is beer." He sent her a pointed look. "And I can't guarantee the temperature."

"Anything above freezing and below the boiling point will do."

Cutter turned toward the small refrigerator, grateful for a moment to cool down. In the two nights since he'd made love to Jessica, his sleep had been sketchy. Whatever parts weren't taken up with erotic dreams of the two of them had been spent reliving the lead-up to his accident. He'd woken repeatedly, heart pumping, body sweating, either from a wicked dream about Jessica or from anticipating his crash.

He was no closer to recovering those missing moments surrounding his wreck. And for the life of him, he couldn't figure out why she'd bolted from his car.

The memory of her taking off—and the old, familiar sensation of being left behind—curdled in his stomach like sour milk as he pulled two bottles of beer from the refrigerator, closing it with a thump.

He twisted off the lids, set her beer on the counter, and tried to pin down the escape artist with his gaze. "I'd love to know where on your long list of rules it states dashing off after sex is polite."

Or that coming back just for a lame publicity stunt was okay. Because when she'd given her reason for returning, he realized he'd been hoping she was here to see him. He gripped his cold bottle.

Man, was he a glutton for punishment.

She nervously feathered her fingers through her hair, the Bambi eyes wary, as if he'd just whipped out a gun. "Dashing off isn't on my list." Color touched her cheeks, making her complexion glow, and a small frown appeared. "Then again, neither is sex just for fun."

His eyebrows shot higher. "Fun?" Of all the things he'd felt while making love to Jessica, lighthearted fun wasn't one of them. "That's not the word I would use." Intense pleasure, yes. Immeasurable satisfaction, absolutely. Life-altering, spine-tingling orgasm, hell yeah.

And being left alone as he watched her take off didn't meet his criteria for fun either.

"I told you before, Cutter," she said. "I don't engage in meaningless sexual exploits."

Meaningless. He leaned closer, his gaze intent on her face, his stomach churning harder now. "Sunshine," he said. "Just because I don't believe in forever doesn't mean what we shared was trivial."

"I didn't say it was trivial."

"Sounds like you did to me."

"You're twisting my words."

He paused, realizing he was asking for more frustration… but he had to know. "Then what is your problem?"

Her lips pressed flat, and her creamy, delicious shoulders slumped a little. "I'm just…" She closed her eyes and rubbed her forehead. "Disappointed in myself."

The statement slammed into him. She wore a look of mis-ery—a feeling he was sure she felt all the way from her sooty black lashes to her pretty, cinnamon-colored toes. And her demeanor made him feel like shit. Just one more layer of hell this lady was heaping upon him.

"Why?" he said.

Cutter waited to hear how he wasn't her usual choice. How a rebelliously bad-mannered, blue-jean-sportin' guy with a surly attitude wasn't on her wish list. Or how she'd always chosen dates like Kevin, successful men who spent their time being nice. Polite. And so charitable they made Cutter's teeth hurt.

"No sex without an emotional investment," she said. The look on her face grew more troubled. "I broke one of my most important rules."

Once again, Jessica's response surprised him, and the doubtful skepticism was hard to contain. "What is it with you and these rules?"

The pulse in her lovely neck bounded hard, as if fighting to break free. "Can we just get on with the competition?"

Cutter stared at her, considering his next move, stumped by her fixation with guidelines that guaranteed to suck all hope for spontaneity in life. The lady was clearly disturbed about their backseat rendezvous, but he was beginning to believe it was about more than *just* him.

And if she insisted on ignoring the issues and proceeding with the competition, so be it.

An idea formed in his head, and he reached into his pocket and pulled out his cellular. "Tell you what." His thumbs wrestled with the tiny keyboard, the weak one on the left and the non-dominant on his right clumsily performing their tasks, but he pushed the irritation aside. "Why don't we let our contestants chime in on the subject?"

Jessica's voice was two octaves higher than normal, with a healthy dose of concern. "What are you typing?"

Cutter finished his text and looked at her. "I asked if an emotional commitment was a requirement for a physical relationship, and why or why not."

She stared at him with such a mixed bag of emotion, Cutter wasn't sure if she was about to laugh, cry or run screaming from the room in frustration.

He knew exactly how she felt.

"Listen…" Cutter slid his phone into his pocket. "I haven't eaten dinner." He picked up the two untouched bottles of beer.

"Let's take our drinks to the kitchen and rummage up some food while we wait for our contestants to respond."

Damage control.

That's what she should be working on. How to fix Cutter's ridiculous post. How to straighten out her life after getting so thoroughly distracted. But even more pressing, how to convince her body to pay attention to all the worries swirling in her head.

Apparently her body refused to care.

Because, after twenty minutes in Cutter's kitchen of rich wood and pricey appliances of stainless steel, Jessica still had no idea how to exercise that damage control. Or had even pondered it, for that matter. But she *had* managed to repeatedly peek at Cutter from the corner of her eye to admire his form. He'd been silently cooking steaks on the indoor grill, infusing the air with the smell of sizzling beef, while she'd been at the granite countertop arranging a salad. But the paucity of fresh vegetables in Cutter's refrigerator was hindering her efforts. She headed for the fridge to make another sweep for something appropriate when she spied a pamphlet on the counter.

Jessica picked up the real-estate brochure with the picture of a sleek, metal warehouse in an upscale industrial park. Intrigued, she finally gathered the courage to break the silence.

She turned to face Cutter. "What is this?"

"It's the building I just bought."

Surprised, she stared at him, the brochure hanging from her fingertips. Property like that cost a hefty sum. Not exactly a purchase one made on a whim. Jessica's curiosity rose exponentially. "What are you going to do with it?"

He continued with his task at the grill. "I'm starting up my own business," he said, as if his statement was no big deal.

But it was. She'd seen the look on his face as he'd struggled to face what came next in his life. When he didn't go on, she said, "Do I at least get to hear what the business is?"

Cutter lifted the steaks onto a plate, set them aside and cut off the grill. "I contacted a buddy of mine who used to work as a mechanic on my team before he retired. Turns out he's bored stiff and ready for some fun." He shifted to face her, leaning a hip against the counter and crossing his arms. With the display of gorgeous muscle, Jessica almost forgot to listen. "I'm going to open a garage that specializes in modifying cars for amateur racers."

She tipped her head curiously. "What kind of modifications?"

"Those that improve the vehicles' performance and efficiency." For the first time since he'd started his story, a spark appeared in his eyes. "Which basically means Karl and I get to soup them up so they go faster."

His first hint of a grin reminded Jessica how devastatingly beautiful he was when he smiled—or came close to smiling, anyway—and she tried hard not to gape at him. She was enormously pleased he was moving on with his life, but she was also taken by his mood. She could sense his anticipation, his excitement about the new opportunity. And the only other time she'd seen those emotions in Cutter was when he'd made love to her.

Hot memories of them steaming up the 'Cuda's windows left Jessica struggling to breathe. She was saved from the treacherous thoughts when Cutter's cellular beeped.

He pulled the phone from his pocket, checking the message. "It's Calamity Jane."

Her heart felt as if it had been tossed an anvil to catch. "Oh, for the love of God," Jessica said. "Not her." When he opened his mouth to speak, she held up a hand. "Don't tell me." She dropped her arm to her side. "You just asked if an emotional commitment was a requirement for a physical relationship." Jessica briefly lifted her gaze heavenward. "Of *course* she said no."

"Technically," he said, his mouth twisting dryly. "Her reply is: *hell no.*"

She narrowed her eyes at him. "Are you two in cahoots?"

His brow crinkled in curiosity. "What do you have against Calamity?"

The question hit too close to home, and she carefully set the brochure clutched in her hand onto the counter, buying some time. Because what was she supposed to say? That the woman made her feel dull? Uninspiring? Because her past sexual experiences, including her marriage, had fallen within the confines of a certain…respectability.

When she looked up, she was surprised to find Cutter now standing two feet away. Jessica's heart rate responded accordingly. His intent expression wasn't reassuring either. There would be no escaping this conversation.

When she didn't answer his question, he tried another. "Why did you take off the other night?" he said.

She'd hoped he'd let the matter slide without further discussion, but that dream died with his words. She should have known he would demand honesty.

"Cutter," she said, leaning her back against the refrigerator. "All my relationships have been with men who have made me feel…" She struggled to find the appropriate word. "Safe," she finally finished. It was the truth, and she had no one to blame except herself, because she'd always chosen her relationships for that very reason. But not this time. She frowned, nibbling on her lip and remembering her cries in the 'Cuda. "But you make me feel…"

When her voice died out a second time, Cutter leaned closer, the proximity doing nothing to ease her heart rate. "Sunshine," he said, his voice low, "what do I make you feel?"

She fought to hold his heated gaze. "Like I don't know what to expect next. I *hate* that feeling."

And exploring the spaces outside her usual safe zone—or more like running around it with scissors in her hand—was too open-ended for comfort.

"I built a whole career out of pushing boundaries," he said. "There is nothing wrong with setting your worries aside and going with your gut."

"Yes," she said adamantly. "There is." His eyes were fixed on her, and he smelled of the musky soap that had filled the 'Cuda when they'd made love. The memory weakened her resolve, and she shifted her gaze to his chin, trying to breathe.

To *think*.

Flustered, Jessica pushed her hair from her forehead, deciding the truth was the only way to go. "I still remember every detail of the day my divorce was finalized." Cutter's body stilled, his face guarded, yet she could tell he was listening carefully. Good. "The lawyer's office was on the top floor of a downtown Miami skyscraper. The sun was shining. The sky was blue. And the view of the Atlantic was beautiful. *Everything* was beautiful, yet I had this horrible, awful feeling of failure. And I was sitting there, amongst all that beauty, thinking…how did this happen?" She fisted her hand, the desolation washing over her again. "I invested fifteen months and worked hard to keep my marriage going. And then it was gone."

"What happened?"

Her gaze drifted to the window overlooking the bay, wishing she knew for certain. Frustrated that she *didn't*. "I think I simply chose poorly, because I needed more from Steve than he had to give, and marriage required more than he wanted to devote to it." She shrugged. "I don't know," she went on, her voice soft. "Maybe we were just too young. Maybe we wanted different things." She returned her gaze to Cutter's. "But in the end, the reason doesn't matter because there was nothing I could do about it."

Just like when her parents had split, and her family—her

life as she'd known it—had been over. She rubbed her brow, as if to erase the memory of the entire fabric of her existence changing, and being powerless to stop it. The terrible feeling of *helplessness*.

She blinked and looked up at him. "So I vowed I'd be more careful in the future. That I wouldn't set myself up for failure again."

And maintaining a measure of control in a relationship was paramount.

"There's a fine line between being cautious and living with restrictive rules that suck the enjoyment from life." He closed a bit of the gap between them. "I think you need to stop analyzing your every move and let go and live a little."

The expression in his eyes set her blood simmering. And it was the cool stainless steel of the refrigerator door at her back that kept her from collapsing.

The beep of a message came again, and Cutter glanced at the phone in his hand. When he looked up, there was a definite light in his eyes as he held up the screen. "Too Hot to Handle's reply."

Requirement is too restrictive a word. Sometimes rules are meant to be broken.

And as Cutter continued to hold her gaze, the look heavy with everything they'd shared and the achy potential for more, Jessica's body burned.

"Cutter," she said, trying to sound confident, her resolve slowly slipping away. "Blindly following your libido isn't a good idea. I've heard the stories." It sounded weak, but she didn't care. "I lead divorce-support groups where people discuss where they went wrong."

His tone left no doubt what he thought of her extracurricular activity. "You volunteer to listen to other people bitch and moan?"

She sent him an overly patient look. "Having a safe place to vent your emotions is healthy."

"Yeah," he said dryly. "But that doesn't mean you have to be the one to listen to it. That's what unsuspecting strangers are for." Cutter's frank gaze scanned her face. "Jessica, you need to relax. Quit being so..." He lifted a hand and traced her collarbone with a finger, sending delicious messages along her nerves. "Focused."

She was focused all right. On his scent. On the seductive feel of his finger. After fifteen months of marriage and two sexual relationships, it wasn't fair that one touch from Cutter lit her up like the neon lights of South Beach at night.

"Or do I have to send you out on another date to get you back in my arms again?" he said.

The sensation of his skin on hers clouded her brain, producing goose bumps and sizzling heat, and understanding rose slowly. Until it toppled over her, and she pressed her back harder against the refrigerator, her voice a squeak. "You were manipulating me?"

"'Course not," he said. His finger explored the sensitive hollow above her collarbone. "I just encouraged you to compare your options." And every one of those men had left her wanting.

More specifically, wanting more of Cutter.

"So what's it going to be?" he said. Cutter's hand paused on the tie at the back of her neck—the one that held up her bodice—and Jessica's heart almost slowed to a stop. "Safety and security?" His green eyes grew dark. "Or a little bit more of the unknown?"

CHAPTER NINE

DESPITE her need for comfortable control, the ache inside Jessica demanded she explore more of the unknown with Cutter. It was either that or therapy—perhaps in a detox facility specializing in brainwashing. Or maybe memory-erasing.

Heart revitalized and now thumping boldly, she stared at him, knowing she was losing the battle. But he'd made her work for him in the car, and then she'd bolted like a coward.

Pride demanded she play this round with more cool.

"Our first time was in a backseat," she said. "And now you're offering me either a countertop or a kitchen table." Not that she'd ever experienced either, but that was irrelevant. She lifted her chin. "My decision would be easier if I was presented with something more original."

Without a word he took hold of her shoulders and turned her around, placing her palms against the refrigerator, like a cop about to frisk her. Her heart rate skyrocketed. Hands covering hers, his hard thighs, chest—and harder erection— pressed against Jessica, enveloping her in steely muscle. Stunned by the wicked sensation, she forgot to breathe.

"Refrigerators are far from standard." His voice went husky at her ear. "But what turns *you* on?"

Paralyzed by an uncontrollable desire for a bad boy, she couldn't reply. And how did one play it cool while oxygen-deficient? Dizzy, she inhaled sharply. "I…"

It was a pathetic effort.

"Come on, Sunshine. For once, apply that honest dialogue to your sex life." His low, rough voice was electrifying. "What does Jessica Wilson fantasize about?"

Her body throbbed. Since they'd made love, her dark dreams had grown more vivid. Detailed. And decadent, leaving her defenseless in their wake. Cutter's form, plastered to her back, triggered her answer. But handing over that much power was impossible. "Nothing."

"Liar." And with that, he tugged on her tie and pushed her dress and panties to the floor. Her thoughts were still spinning from the sudden turn of events when Cutter shifted her two steps to the right, replanting her hands against the freezer side of the fridge. "Stay here."

And then he moved away.

Dumbfounded, Jessica blinked, feeling ridiculous wearing nothing but high heels, hands braced against an appliance. Relieved he'd let his question go, she peeked over her shoulder as Cutter returned with a dishtowel, and her eyebrows drew together in question.

He paused behind her, his gaze intense. "Do you trust me?"

Unnerved, struggling for air, she hesitated…and realized the answer was yes. The irreverent rebel was too bold, too blunt and occasionally rude, but he wouldn't hurt her.

When she nodded, Cutter said, "If we break your need for safety and security, I might get an answer to my question." He covered her eyes with the makeshift blindfold, tying it behind her head.

Sweat pricked her temples. "Cutter…" The word ended with a nervous laugh. Unable to see, she heard the refrigerator open beside her, bottles being shuffled and then the door closed. What had she signed on for? "Cutter?" her nerves stretched with curiosity and apprehension, feeling exposed. "What are you doing?"

"Starting with my fantasy about you."

Thick liquid sloshed in a container, and Jessica's stomach flopped. "That better not be hot sauce."

A rusty chuckle came from behind. "Nope." Cutter swept her hair aside. "I've thought about this since I tasted your creamy vanilla shoulders at the Aquarium."

Jessica smelled chocolate before she felt a cool drizzle on a shoulder. His finger smoothed the slick circle, sensitizing her skin, which grew worse when his mouth sampled his creation.

"Definitely the right mix of flavors," he rumbled against her.

She swallowed hard. "I think chocolate syrup qualifies as a cliché."

"Yeah." He removed his mouth from her shoulder. "It's a good one, too."

Enclosed in the dark, she wondered what would come next. Her muscles tensed when a wet finger touched her back, tracing syrup between her shoulder blades, and his mouth followed to clean the mess, searing her skin. After a pause, a chocolaty dollop hit the opposing shoulder, lips nibbling next, and Jessica sucked in a breath. A brief lull…and a syrupy finger slicked down the curve of her waist, a tongue licked it clean and perspiration pricked Jessica's neck.

Desire spiraled higher as, between each of Cutter's choices, Jessica tensed, vulnerable and sightless—waiting for what would follow. The sweet smell of chocolate, the sound of her harsh breathing and the scrape of Cutter's teeth filled her heightened senses. As the pleasure curled tighter, her visionless world condensed to the feel of Cutter, her body's response and the cool refrigerator beneath her palms.

With each new spot, he moved lower, until her body was singing. When he knelt on the floor behind her, her head spun.

"What do you dream about?" Cutter drew a line of chocolate up one buttock, across the small of her back, and down the other cheek. And then he held her hips, feeding on her flesh with his lips, tongue and teeth. Driving her mad.

Engulfing her in flames.

By the end, Jessica's need was urgent. Stronger than any reservations. More powerful than her need to maintain a little control. Cutter stood and wrapped his arms around her, his hard body plastered behind hers. One hand on her breast, teasing the tip, the other stroked between her thighs, an agonizing pressure building as hot moisture made his fingers slick.

His tone was sinfully dark. "What qualifies as original to Jessica Wilson?"

Blindfolded, trembling and desperate, the last of her cool slipped, and she gave in to the desire, pressing back against his hard shaft. "This."

Cutter went still, obviously not following her vague answer. And then understanding filled his tone. "You mean this position."

A flush heated her face. Embarrassingly enough, it was just that simple. "Yes."

Without a word, Cutter released his zipper and kneed her thighs apart. Breath frozen, heart bashing her ribs, she tipped her hips back to meet him, and Cutter plunged inside her wet folds.

With a gasp of shocked pleasure, she arched her back, damp palms braced against the chilled stainless steel in front of her. Cutter wrapped his arms back around her, leaning over her, thrusting deep again and again, fingers stroking her between the legs. His free hand captured her jaw, turned her mouth to meet his. Hard, chocolaty lips devoured hers in a moist, open-mouthed kiss.

It was just as delicious as she'd imagined, as decadent as she'd dreamed, smashing her last thoughts of control. Defenseless, caught in his strong embrace, Jessica turned herself over to the wickedly primitive need as Cutter consumed her from behind.

"Tell me again why I'm here?" Cutter said into his cellular.

Jessica's chuckle was low in his ear. "The celebrity originally scheduled to appear for the Battle of the Sexes photo op had to cancel." Her voice sounded amused. "And *you* volunteered to come in his place."

"Oh, yeah." Cutter gripped his phone. "Remind me to be more careful when you're naked in my bed." Hoping to spot Jessica, he wove his way through the throng of locals filling the new gymnasium at the Boys and Girls Club, all funded by Jessica's ex. Bleachers lined two sides, with basketball hoops mounted at either end. On the polished maple floor of the court, round tables had been set up for the grand opening dinner.

"How did the photo op go?" she said.

"I sidestepped the reporter's questions and smiled for the camera."

"You smiled?"

Cutter bit back the grin and finally spied Jessica across the crowd. Cellphone pressed against her ear, she was dressed in a denim skirt that ended a tantalizing several inches above the knees and dainty flat sandals. Despite the casual attire, she managed to look as beautiful as she had in her formal wear.

The long expanse of bare legs was definitely a winner in his book.

"Could be *smile* is an exaggeration," he said. "But I definitely managed not to be disagreeable. Which is amazing considering the torture this event is turning out to be." He threaded his way through the people and leaned against the basketball pole, ten feet from Jessica and her gorgeous display of legs. "I wouldn't have volunteered if I'd known I still had to keep my hands to myself in public."

Jessica's eyes found his from across the crowd, and she sent him a sultry smile. Despite the distance, the effect was like a wrecking ball to the gut. "As far as the guests are concerned," she said. "I'm here with Steve." She turned to the wall plastered with the simplistic artwork of kids. Hand prints. Stick figures. And the swirls of abstract finger paints. "And *we* are just friends. So remember," she went on, her voice low and exquisitely sexy, "no touching."

In the past three days and two delicious nights, they'd done a lot of touching.

After the interlude at his refrigerator, the online flirting they'd finished with the contestants had been the most stimulating to date. But trying to keep his mind on their task—much less his comments PG-rated—was damn near impossible with her lounging naked in his bed.

He looked at the poster Jessica was pretending to examine. Even from a distance, it was obvious it was by a small child, the features on the face grossly out of proportion. "That one is definitely a Picasso in the making." The responding chuckle in his ear was low. Her gauzy, off-the-shoulder blouse exposed the creamy shoulders, and the memory of the taste of her skin set his body on fire. "It's killing me that I can't touch you."

"It'll be good for you." She targeted him with her wide, brown gaze, her face glowing with humor. "Encourage a little self-discipline."

A couple strolled between them, and he waited until his line of sight cleared before speaking. "Problem is," he said. "I have none around you. And that blouse isn't helping."

"Cutter," she said. "Stop looking at me like that."

"No one knows we're talking to each other." He turned to lean his back against the pole, eyes scanning the crowd, but unable to prevent them from returning to the beautiful woman. And even though it was impossible, he swore he smelled her delicate scent. Or maybe after the past three days it was simply seared into his memory. "I figured out your smell."

She turned her profile to him, examining another poster on the wall. "What are you talking about?"

"Sweet, with a hint of cinnamon," he said. "It reminds me of apple cider."

Christ, when had he started sounding so romantic?

"That's my shampoo," she said.

He looked at her again, the woman who, if he wasn't careful, would soon have him spouting compliments and smiling like a moron. He still couldn't figure out why making love to her was different. "Can't I at least meet you secretly behind the bleachers? Just a quick kiss and a grope to get me through until dinner?"

She wrinkled her nose in what looked like an amused grimace. "FYI, the word *grope* is never associated with anything appealing."

"Is *fondle* better?"

"Most women would prefer the term *caress*."

He gripped his cellular and looked back at the crowd milling about, trying to pretend the beautiful lady didn't have his total attention. "*Caress* isn't in my vocabulary. But I'll agree to the term if you'll agree to my offer of a secret meeting."

"Not going to happen, Mr. Wildcard," she said. "We'll sit at Steve's table for dinner. But that's it for the contact."

He pursed his lips and deliberately dropped his voice to a suggestive tone. "Not even if I promise to do something spectacularly original to you?"

There was a pause on the line, and Jessica turned to look at him. Even from ten feet away he could see her gaze was hot. Every cell in his body was blitzed with an energy that left him sizzling, as if he'd been shoved in a microwave set on high.

Her voice was husky. "In that case, I might be open to hearing about your plans."

A bonfire set up residence in his gut and spread lower, and Cutter could practically see the sparks arcing in the air between them.

"Jess," a masculine voice called.

Beating his libido into submission, Cutter hit the disconnect button on his cellular and watched Jessica's ex approach her as she slipped her phone into her purse. Dressed in a sharp navy suit, Steve Brice still looked relaxed enough to blend in with the casual crowd. The dark-haired man stopped and kissed Jessica on the cheek. When Steve's gaze caught Cutter's, he steered Jessica in Cutter's direction.

"Good to see you again," Steve said as he stuck out his hand.

"Nice gym." Cutter returned the handshake.

Steve gave a no-big-deal shrug. "It helps keep the kids out of trouble."

Cutter's lips twisted at the irony. "I'm sure the community appreciates your efforts. I would have been better off spending time at my local Boys and Girls Club as a boy." Would have made his mother happy, too. She'd made it clear she'd never wanted him, and had lived to get her moody teen out of the house, not caring where he was…as long as it was somewhere else. "'Course, by the time I had my driver's license, proving I had the fastest car in the neighborhood was my only goal."

Truthfully, getting away from home had been his initial goal. And then he'd hooked up with a crowd of racers, discovering the thrill of high speeds. Beating the competition. *Winning.* The only worries he'd had were his opponent and the possibility of dying. The first had driven him to go faster.

The second hadn't scared him at all.

Steve smiled. "The whole point of the club is to keep the kids *off* the streets."

"True," Cutter said. He let out a wry scoff. "But I never was much for conformity."

The man's grin grew bigger, and his sidelong glance at his ex was less than subtle. "And how's that working out for you now?"

Cutter did his best to keep the smile from his face. "So far so good."

"You haven't caved under the pressure?" Steve said.

Cutter's lips twisted in amusement. "Not yet." Though his thoughts about Jessica's scent did make his response questionable.

Jessica glanced suspiciously from Cutter and then back to Steve. "What exactly are we discussing here?"

"I'm not sure," Steve said with a grin.

She shot Cutter a this-better-not-be-about-me look as her ex went on.

"I've got to go get this dinner started with a speech." Steve jerked his head in the direction of a podium along the far wall, amusement dancing in his eyes. "I'll let you two get back to your phone conversation now."

Steve headed off, and Cutter turned to Jessica, trying to decide which he liked more…the old standby roll-of-her-eyes-heavenward or the I-was-so-right look currently inhabiting her face now.

But he had no regrets about the phone call. "Smug becomes you."

"I knew we were being too obvious."

"How about we play footsy under the dinner table instead?"

She shot him a faux menacing look. "Only if you promise to be discreet."

"Sunshine, Mr. Discretion is my other nickname."

She turned and headed for their table, shooting him an amused, doubtful expression over her shoulder. "Come on, Wildcard. Let's see if you can live up to that misnomer."

Cutter clearly was trying to make her pay for her teasing comment.

With Steve to her left, and Cutter to her right, Jessica tried to pay attention to the conversation at the table. But it was difficult to follow the discussion with Cutter's hand on her knee. He was debating the present-day status of racing with the man sitting beside him, and all the while his thumb was stroking her thigh beneath the curtain of the tablecloth.

It made focusing impossible; she was unable to get past the delicious circles he was drawing on the skin just above her knee.

The smell of rich, spicy tomato sauce seeped into her consciousness, and Jessica finally noticed the man delivering food to a nearby group of guests. But, on closer inspection, he wasn't a man. It was a pimply-faced adolescent. She managed to refocus on her surroundings and saw a dozen or so teens, all wearing black jeans and white shirts, carrying out trays laden with plates of lasagna, distributing them to the tables.

Cutter leaned in to address Steve, allowing his tormenting hand to conveniently inch a fraction higher up her leg. Jessica shot him a warning look, but, without even a glance in Jessica's direction, Cutter addressed her ex. "I was expecting pizza or hamburgers."

Clearly oblivious to Jessica's predicament, Steve said, "The local Italian restaurant donated the food, and the teens at the club volunteered to serve the dinner."

Cutter's fingers reached her inner thigh, blistering her skin, and her heart pumped harder, sweat dotting the nape of her neck as the conversation between the two men blurred.

This kind of behavior was exactly what she'd expected from a rebel bad boy. She *should* be disturbed by the illicit thrill shooting through her veins. But she hadn't counted on enjoying the clandestine caresses of one man while the table guests assumed she was here with another.

Lovely. Next she'd be changing her slogan from 'fostering honest dialogue in finding The One' to a women's-magazine version of 'how to kink up your sex life.'

And she was beginning to question her skepticism of

Calamity Jane, because Cutter put out her fire like no man ever had.

"Mr. Thompson?" a voice called, interrupting the conversation.

Jessica looked up to see a teen who looked vaguely familiar. Shaggy dark hair brushed his shoulders, and his oversize jeans hung low on his hips, the waistband of his orange boxers barely peeking above the denim. The brown eyes were still dark, but the belligerent look from the photo Jessica had shown Cutter was tempered with an emotion that surprised her.

Adoration.

The teen stuck out a paper napkin and a pen towards Cutter. "Can I have your autograph?"

Cutter's thumb ceased its disturbing caress, and his grip on her leg grew tight with tension. She shot him a curious look, and the expression on his face was a shock. She'd seen him on TV in the past, meeting and greeting kids, and he'd always been friendly.

But this time, he had a faint frown.

Cutter's head thumped with a familiar, gnawing pain, and he stared at the kid who looked barely old enough to shave. It took five seconds for full recognition to trigger his memory.

Emmanuel. The adolescent dropout. Big fan of the Wildcard. The belligerent teen who'd gone back to finish high school with the goal of following in Cutter Thompson's footsteps.

Damn. Why would the kid still want to be a screwup like him?

Years of experience had trained Cutter how to deal with fans, but he hated the goofy, almost fanatical expression the teen was wearing. Hadn't the kid heard the news? That Cutter had pulled a reckless stunt that cost him his career?

He beat back the urge to tell the boy to scram. Struggling

to take control of his suddenly sour mood, Cutter paused until he couldn't stand the hero worship on the adolescent's face any longer.

"Sure, kid," he said gruffly. He did his best not to snatch the napkin from the boy, to hurry the process along. But the need to get him to move on about his business was hard to suppress. After scribbling his signature, he stuck the paper out, hoping this would be the end of it.

But Emmanuel, wannabe Cutter Thompson, wasn't done yet.

"I watched you bump Chester Coon on TV," he said, taking the napkin back. Cutter's head thumped harder, the pain piercing, and a wave of nausea hit as the kid continued, his eyes glowing with excitement. "Dude, it was freakin' awesome!" he said, pumping the air with a fist that was like a head-on collision with Cutter's head. "The way you slid across the finish line on your roof. *Sweet!* And still pulled off second place, too."

Bile rose in Cutter's throat as memory engulfed him, and he was back in the stock car. He could smell burning rubber, feel the heart-pounding speed, his fingers gripping the wheel.

Oblivious, Emmanuel went on, his eyes shining with hero worship. "And you were the only one brave enough to take on that dirtbag Chester Coon."

Brave.

Sweat broke out on Cutter's lip, but the teen continued with his relentless, blow-by-blow account. His whole face lit with a smile, Emmanuel said, "And you so totally *owned* that track—"

The searing pain of his crash hit like a sledgehammer. "Hey," Cutter interjected, his voice low, body seized by ache and memory. "Don't you have other guests to serve?"

Through the haze of agony, Cutter watched the kid step

back, the excitement wiped from his face. "Sure." Emmanuel's face was nonchalant, his eyes flat. "Sure thing, man."

The teen turned and headed off, and Cutter fought the violent urge to vomit. Because the kid had called him *brave*. But Cutter knew better.

In truth, maybe he'd always known better.

Head pounding with the return of his memories of the crash, he watched Emmanuel walk away with his shoulders hunched, and the cauldron of dark emotion boiled higher in Cutter's gut, charring his insides. He recognized the blank look on the kid's face. Cutter had worn it a million times himself. And the adoration, too. But his father hadn't deserved his hero worship, and Cutter sure as hell didn't deserve Emmanuel's now.

He closed his eyes as his memories of the wreck, his *emotions,* came tumbling back. There had been no self-sacrifice on his part. Cutter had simply been incensed at Chester Coon's gall, threatened by the driver's hard racing as he'd challenged Cutter for the lead. Because…that track had been *Cutter's.*

He'd taken a risky move, had lost his career, all because of his anger and conceit.

The aroma of lasagna, which had smelled so mouthwatering before, almost finished him off. Battling the nausea that was growing hotter by the minute, Cutter slowly became aware of the rest of the table.

Jessica was staring at him, wide-eyed, with a look of pure disappointment on her face, and Cutter's stomach took on the festering essence of a primordial ooze. Poisoning him from the inside out.

Shit.

She finally spoke, her tone low and laced with disapproval. "What was that all about?"

He forced his expression to remain neutral. "What?"

Jessica turned in her seat to face him. "You just crushed that kid's heart."

Amidst all the roiling emotions, another stab of guilt slashed deep. He dropped his eyes to the table and reached for his glass of iced tea, his hand clammy. "I doubt that."

"Oh, *please*."

Cutter cleared his throat, shifting in his seat, suppressing the need to bolt. To *run* from the bitter truth. But Jessica was waiting for a response, so he tried to give her one. "Even if I did, he'll get over it." He glanced at her from the corner of his eye, and her feelings were stamped clearly in her posture. Her back looked as if she had just traded her spine for an axle.

And although her words came out quietly, the low tone did nothing to detract from their impact. "That boy looks up to you."

Cutter gripped his tea glass, his fingertips blanching from the pressure, resisting the urge to crush the glass with his hand. Or at least hurl it against the wall. But he couldn't do that. Because here he sat, fool that he was, next to Jessica at this quaint little community party.

A brand-spanking-new gymnasium—funded by her honorable ex-husband—and full of nothing but do-gooders and one adoring, deluded juvenile fan.

And then there was him. Cutter Thompson.

Just who the hell was *he?*

He sucked in a breath and then quietly blew it out, loosening his grip on his drink, forcing himself to let it all go. He'd built a life out of not caring what people thought. It was how he'd survived. "Since when is some kid's misplaced idol worship *my* problem?"

Anger clouded her eyes. "But you at least have to try—"

"Sunshine," he said, cutting her off, aware of the stares of their table companions as the two of them argued. He couldn't take it anymore, hating the look of utter disenchantment in her face. But he hadn't asked for the teenager's hero-worship. He used to want it. But not anymore. He used to think he deserved it.

And it was a hell of a thing to look back on his career and realize he *didn't*.

"I don't owe anybody anything," he said. Her flush grew brighter as he continued. "And just because some starry-eyed kid—"

She held up her hand. "That starry-eyed kid needs as many positive male influences in his life as he can get," she said, staring at him. "He's growing up without a father." His conscience took another thrashing, and Jessica's tone was laced with accusation. "Which means you, of *all* people, should be extra kind."

Extra kind?

He raised an eyebrow. "Sunshine," he said softly. Her persistent optimism defied reason. "Do you think the rest of the world is gonna treat him with kid gloves because of his crappy childhood?" She frowned, a small furrow appearing between her brows, and he knew she knew the answer was no. "Exactly," he said.

Cutter had learned it over and over again. And just when he'd thought he couldn't take any more, the world had turned around and kicked him in the ass again. And as a teen he'd raced those cars, angry and getting into trouble, until he'd learned that no one cared. But he hadn't really learned anything. Because he'd let his anger control him again...and lost his racing career.

And there was no undoing that now.

With a defeated sigh, he passed a frustrated hand through his hair. "The kid might as well learn that when life sucks, you just have to deal with it."

Her face grew dark. "That's a horrible—"

"That's right," Cutter said as he stood, his chair scraping on the wood floor, the need to retreat overwhelming him. "It *is* horrible." He looked down on Miss Perpetual Pollyanna. "Life can *be* horrible." They stared at each other for a moment longer, until Cutter went on. "I'm not hungry," he said, tossing his napkin on his empty plate. "Enjoy your meal."

CHAPTER TEN

THE next afternoon Jessica made her way around the side of Cutter's house, sandals crunching on the sunlight-dappled gravel walk. His sports car was parked in the driveway, so she knew he was home. But he wasn't answering her knock at the front door. Which meant he was either in the backyard…

Or he was refusing to talk to her. With Cutter, you just never knew.

Gnawing on her lower lip, she rounded the corner of the house and spied him by the pool, hosing off the deck. Her stomach vaulted, flipped and then landed. Only now it was positioned lower in her abdomen. She stopped and let the sight of swaying palms, green grass and the sea-green waters of Biscayne Bay beyond soothe her nerves. Which would have worked if the handsome man had been dressed in more than a bathing suit, chest and legs exposed.

And if the memory of how they had ended last night wasn't embossed in her brain.

If ever there was a sign that Cutter Thompson was the kind of man she needed to stay away from, she now had proof. After he'd cut that poor boy off at his knees, and Cutter's face had closed down, it had taken Jessica about two seconds to realize that he had emotionally and mentally checked out.

Problems? Time to clam up. Bothered about something? Insult someone and retreat into your emotion-free hole. It didn't take a doctorate in psychology—or even regular viewing of the daytime TV talk shows—to realize that in every relationship, he would do the same thing.

Steve hadn't been fond of expressing himself either, and Jessica was one-hundred-percent sure that it had been the beginning of the end of their marriage. But even at his worst, Steve had never been this reticent. He'd even been willing to marry her.

And he would *never* treat someone as callously as Cutter had Emmanuel.

Last night Jessica had gone to bed livid, woken up disturbed and then spent the rest of the day trying to sort through her emotions. Which was a frustratingly difficult task. Because when it came to her feelings about the man standing on the teak deck, Jessica vacillated wildly. It was like riding a pendulum, swinging back and forth, trying to figure out when it would stop. She just wasn't clear if, when the pendulum finally came to a halt, she'd even *like* the real Cutter Thompson.

Lovely. Wasn't that a depressing thought?

Water jetted from the hose, hitting the wood with a forceful stream as Cutter herded the leaves from the pool area and under the tall hedge that provided a living privacy fence. Jessica smoothed her hand down her peasant blouse, steadying her nerves, and stepped up onto the deck.

Cutter shot her a glance and then returned his gaze to his task, his expression still shuttered.

Nice, this should go well.

"You here to read me the riot act again?" he asked.

Jessica curled her fingers against her shorts. "No," she said, crossing closer to him. "I came to discuss our plan for the last session." Among other things, but she wasn't sure how to broach the subject of Emmanuel. Easing into it seemed best. "I want to make sure we end the publicity stunt on the right note."

He lifted a brow, and Jessica was stumped. The facial cue could have meant anything. Was he questioning her topic, or waiting for her to explain what note she wanted to achieve? Or perhaps, considering the way things had ended between them last night, he was simply noting the irony of her statement.

She let out a quiet sigh and gave up on the impossible task of translating his expression. "Steve and I discussed you after you left the gym."

After a brief pause, he released the lever on the hose, shutting off the water, and turned to face her. Despite the guarded look in Cutter's eyes, he didn't ask what they had talked about. She suspected he was too proud to ask.

Or maybe he didn't care.

But she told him anyway. "Steve read *me* the riot act and said I should cut you some slack." She chewed on her lip before going on. "He also said I was wrong for calling you out in public like that."

Cutter gave a nonchalant shrug and depressed the handle again, eyes on the aim of his hose. "We didn't raise our voices. It wasn't a big scene."

It had felt *massive* to her, and his insistence on treating it with a casual air made the nervous tension worse instead of better. But the cool mist created by the spray of water felt good. She gave a halfhearted lift of her shoulder. "Better than getting caught making out behind the bleachers." Her stomach clenched.

She shouldn't have said that.

But at least she finally got an authentic response, the old Cutter reappearing with a dry twist of an amused mouth. "Sunshine, if anything, our fight just *confirmed* we're sleeping together."

This surprised her. "Do you always get into fights with the women you're involved with?"

"I've never been involved with someone quite so demanding before."

She hiked a brow dryly. "They must not have expected much."

"I guess I had other things to recommend me. It certainly wasn't my sparkling charm."

Despite her nerves, and the crackling tension, heat flared in her belly. Oh yeah, she'd been privy to a good bit of the things he did well. Had tossed every one of her plans aside when she'd signed on for more.

The tangle of emotions in her chest grew tighter, cinching into a knot.

"Have you *ever* been charming?" she said.

Cutter turned his hose on the next section of the deck, and the pause lengthened, filled only with the sound of water beating on wood. The moment stretched so long, Jessica thought he wasn't going to respond. But when she was about to ask again, Cutter finally spoke.

"I spent my preteen and teenage years angry at the world. Angry at my dad for leaving. I was even angry at my mom." He cut her a sideways glance. "It didn't leave much room for charm."

She studied him. The similarities between Cutter and the sullen teen from last night were impossible to ignore. And that seemed a nice segue into making that point to the stubborn man. "I'm sure Emmanuel feels the same way."

"He's just doing his time. He's *supposed* to be pissed off at the world."

"Fine. So he's dutifully being the sullen and disagreeable teen. But you are an *adult*." She swept a lock of hair from her damp cheek, the bright sun and her nerves heating her skin, and sent him a pointed look. "You should be better than that by now."

He stared at her for a long moment before answering. "Yeah," he said, his voice even. "Maybe I should."

His tone wasn't thoughtful in an I'm-contemplating-changing-my-ways fashion, it was more of a statement of fact. As if he knew how he was supposed to behave, yet still refused to comply. Cutter Thompson apparently didn't conform, no matter *what*.

She watched him return to his task of wielding the hose, driving the sprigs of greenery off the deck edge. Unsure where to go next, she said, "I watched the wreck again."

It had been disturbing to scrutinize, inch by pixilated inch, the stock car spin out, flip onto its back and slide across the track before busting into the wall, scattering parts across the pavement, all the while knowing Cutter had been inside. As a fan, it had been horrifying. Now that she knew him personally, it was terrifying. Because it made her realize she was beginning to *care* about him. The thought scared her senseless. And, ultimately, this conversation was about one thing.

She desperately needed to believe he was better than his actions last night.

"You're lucky to be alive," she said.

"You think I don't know that?"

She shook her head softly. "I honestly don't know what you think or feel." She was still trying to figure it out.

Still trying to figure *him* out. Because being with a guy who was the antithesis of everything she'd ever hoped for was wringing her emotions dry. She was now running around outside that comfort zone with those sharp scissors aimed at her heart.

When he didn't respond, Jessica stepped closer, staring at his profile. Because, bitter or not, the way Cutter had treated Emmanuel was wrong. Okay, so she should have discussed it with him in private, but that didn't excuse his behavior.

"Sometimes you have to take the higher road, Cutter," she said. His movements slowed, as if listening, but he kept his attention on his task. "Be the better person," she continued. "Yes, I realize it was painful hearing a tactless reminder about your crash. What you've lost." She hooked her hands on her hips, wanting him to recognize why she had been so disappointed in him. "But Emmanuel is just a seventeen-year-old kid. You can't expect him to comprehen—"

"It's not just about *what* I lost," Cutter said, cutting her and the hose off at the same time. "It's about *why*."

Confusion forced her brow downward. "I don't understand." As she stood there, studying his expression, it dawned on her what he meant. "You got your memory back."

"Yes." He tossed the hose onto the teak wood and it landed with a thunk. "I did," he said, and then he strode to the far end of the deck. He turned to face her, his expression hard. "In a fit of ego, I decided a rookie needed a lesson. Not to remind him of the rules so it's safer for everybody. And not just to win a single event." He jabbed his thumb at his chest. "I did it to show him that that track was *mine*." The arrogant words, the bluntly honest look on his face, sank her stomach lower in her belly, leaving her stunned as he went on. "He threatened my number-one status so I wanted to teach him a lesson. But what I got was an injury that guaranteed I'd never race again." He turned his face away from her, his profile lit by the bright sunlight, his expression harsh.

When she finally found her voice, it felt weak. "*That's* why you bumped Chester Coon?"

He passed a hand down his face, as if fatigued, but his words were no less candid. "Yes. It was all about *me*," he said. "Most people would say I got what I deserved. Ruining my own career." Cutter looked at her again, not bothering to hide the fiery emotion. "And it just so happens…I agree." She could hear the regret in his tone, see the stark expression on his face before it went bitter. "So I damn sure don't want any misplaced idolism from a kid searching for a father figure via a has-been sports star."

She blinked. "Maybe your memory is wrong. Maybe you—"

"No, Jessica," he said. "It's not."

It took a moment for the reality to fully sink in. And she shook her head, trying to wrap her head around the news. "It was just one split-second stupid mistake. It doesn't mean that you're unworthy of the kid's respect—"

"Christ, Jessica," Cutter said, frustration filling his face. "Don't start reading something into this that isn't there." The frown grew deeply skeptical. "This isn't about some pity-party, talk-show feeling of unworthiness." He stepped closer, exchanging cynicism for callous candor. "It is about my actions *being* unworthy."

She blew out a breath. After crossing her arms, she studied him carefully, trying to make sense of his words. To sort it all out. But it didn't compute. "You were the number-one driver for *six years.* You had to work like a dog to get to the top. And even harder to stay there. It took discipline and determination. One impulsive mistake does not erase everything that you've accomplished." She was feeling more confident in her words, but he was still looking at her as if about to refute her claim, so she continued. "Especially considering that, during all your years of hard work, while at the top of your game, you made sure your sponsors supported the causes that were important to you."

"That was just business."

"You chose to single out kids in need as your focus," she said. "I don't think that was a coincidence."

"Sunshine." He stared at her as if she were a new flavor of crazy. "The only humanitarian around here is you."

She was one-hundred-percent convinced his choice of charities was influenced by his childhood. He might not be able to see it, but *she* could. "I hate to break it to you, Mr. Thompson," she said. "You do have a few nice-guy qualities. Good-guy qualities."

He reached out and gripped her wrist, his voice low. "Cut it out."

Heart pounding in her chest, she stared up at him. He stepped closer, and the moment lengthened until Jessica thought it would squeal in protest from the stretch.

The hard look in Cutter's gaze didn't budge, but his voice turned deceptively quiet. "You were so mad at me after Emmanuel left I knew I'd never get to touch you again. Which would have been just as well."

They were the very words she'd been telling herself all day, yet the need that engulfed her now was stronger, and her whole world converged on the hand around her wrist. With one touch, he made her doubt her decisions. She should agree with him. Tell him he was right. But she couldn't do it. The muscles in her throat contracted, making her voice tight. "It wouldn't have been just as well."

He continued, his tone serious. And deliberate. "But I'm still the same person now as I was last night, Jessica." His fingers on her wrist were firm. "And I am *not* going to continue having sex with a woman who twists me into something I'm not, just so you can feel better about sleeping with me."

Denial surged. "What are you talking about? I don't do that."

"Sunshine—" he pulled her another half step closer, and her heart moved closer to her throat "—you just did."

Her breaths came shallow and fast, the intensity in his stare pinning her to the ground. "I never said—"

"You say I was an insensitive jerk to Emmanuel, and most people would agree," he said, his voice now dangerously low. "It wasn't my first mistake in your eyes, and it won't be the last. But you either want to be with me or you don't. And you can't divide people up into black and white, good or bad."

Her mouth dropped open. "That's not what I'm trying to do."

The frustration on his face was profound. "Then what *are* you trying to do?"

Her mind swimming, she blurted out the truth. "I'm trying to figure out who you are."

"You don't want to know."

But she did—because she'd fallen so completely under his spell. One touch and she chucked all her goals out the door. And she couldn't figure out *why*.

"Yes," she said firmly. "I want to know."

Cutter's face went rock-solid. "Fine. I told you that first day in my garage, but I'll spell it out for you again." He pulled her another half step closer. "I was a cocky, arrogant bastard. I enjoyed the public's attention. And I loved signing photographs." His words were blunt, his tone firm. "I chose the charities, yes, but the real kick for me was the interaction with the fans." He lifted an eyebrow for emphasis. "And that was ninety-eight percent about stroking my ego. Because I liked the way it made *me* feel." He paused, as if allowing time for the heavy words to sink further to the bottom of her heart. "The remaining two percent was to please the sponsors. For me, it's always been about the angle."

She pressed her eyes closed, trying to take it all in. But the truth was too awful to comprehend. "Is that it?" she said softly, lifting her lids and scanning his face. "Is that all there is to you?"

Something flashed in his eyes she couldn't interpret. "Even I haven't figured that out. But let me tell you what I *do* know," he said, pulling her until they were almost toe to toe. "I'm a shade of gray, Jessica. Darker on some days, lighter on others. But the real question is..." He lowered his head, his face only inches from hers. "Is that good enough for Jessica Wilson to sleep with or not?"

She stared into those sea-green eyes so turbulent with frustration. Resentment. And at the heart of it...desire. His fingers were warm on her wrist, but her skin burned. His musky scent, his presence, swamping her in a sensual fog. There was no redeeming feature about his past. He was all about Cutter. His actions had been selfish through and through.

But God help her, she still wanted him.

The sensual fog closed in around her, and she was powerless to stop it. "Yes."

He pulled her arm, and her body collided with his, his mouth crashing into hers. An instant battle for supremacy, with Cutter the clear winner. He took what he wanted, not looking for submission, simply demanding she keep up. Barely leaving her room to breathe.

He was giving her a full taste of what she'd been fantasizing about since she'd watched his crash again last night. She'd been horrified by the sight. Grateful he was alive. And she was still angry at him for letting her down. But she was also disappointed in herself for wanting him—whoever he was—and *this,* despite his actions.

The power, the pace of the kiss was exhilarating. A slice of the out-of-control passion he'd only hinted at in the past. The kind she'd never experienced before, had never really wanted in a man.

Until she met him.

She clung to his upper arms, trying to steady herself under the onslaught. Cutter had one hand behind her head, sealing her mouth to his, while his other yanked at their clothes. His biceps alternately bulged and lengthened beneath her hands as he pulled on buttons and zippers, impatiently sweeping the fabric aside. When she tried to help, desperate to make it happen, her hands kept getting in the way, and wound up hindering his efforts instead of helping.

"Don't," he said, his voice gruff, pushing her hand away.

Jessica abandoned the plan, and he pulled off her shirt. He clasped her face, pulling her lips back to his, and she met him now, taste for taste. Her passion was running at high speed, catching up with him. She ran her hands down his chest, his skin hot, yet damp. The chest hair crisp beneath her fingers.

Cutter pushed her shorts and his swimsuit down, and the fabric dropped to the teak at their feet.

And as he backed her towards the lounge chair behind her, both stepping out of their clothes, they stumbled back in a tangle of legs and lips. Cutter stuck out an arm, catching their drop onto the chaise, cushioning their fall. He landed on top of her, not missing a beat, continuing his full-speed-ahead clip. If anything, as if sensing she'd caught up, he shifted into higher gear.

It was maddeningly intense.

His hands and mouth were everywhere, her breasts, her stomach, between her thighs. Caressing, kissing, nipping and then moving on, leaving her in a breathless daze, trying to match his pace. Overwhelmed by the barrage of sensations. As her skin burned from his tongue, the rasp of his chin and from the hot sun blaring down on them, Cutter consumed her as if she was in danger of disappearing if he slowed down. All the rough, raw edges present since the day they'd first met highlighted in bold.

It was as if he was determined to show her the full force of the darker shade of Cutter Thompson.

Hands on her hips, he nipped his way up her belly, her breasts, and took her mouth as, in one swift movement, Cutter arched his hips, driving deep into her. Jessica cried out in relief.

He paused, capturing her head between his hands, and looked down on her, his face close. Her mind spinning, she gazed into his hard eyes, the steel muscles of his thighs pressed between the soft inner of her own.

Hands on her head, Cutter began to move between her legs. Swift. Sure. No holding back and no apologies. Taking what he wanted. A massive force of need.

But she hadn't counted on feeding his need being a catalyst for her own. His earlier frustration and his overwhelming desire stamped his every move. She arched beneath him, her hips meeting his, the sensual haze tightening her muscles in anticipation yet turning her body to gel. She clung to his arms, his muscles hard beneath her fingers, her body insisting she comply.

His gaze bored into hers as his movements swept her along in an undertow that sucked her down, skirting the edges between dark desire and danger, threatening to close over her head. She felt as if she'd stepped into the deep end of a pool of need, barely able to touch the bottom with her tiptoes, struggling to keep her face above water. To breathe.

She shut her eyes as the pool climbed higher, closing over her head, cutting off everything but her ability to feel the pleasure taking root in her body. Until she finally went under, vibrant bits of light bursting behind her eyelids as she came, the violent shocks gripping her body.

The sun bore down on Cutter's back as he gradually became aware of his surroundings. His chest heaved with every breath, his muscles were spent. His ribs ached and his left arm burned. Sweat trickled down his back, and his thighs felt slick between Jessica's. He opened his eyes to the sight of her face, lids closed, cheeks flushed. Her temples were damp, dark hair stuck to her skin.

She'd never looked more beautiful, and the terrible reality of what they'd shared clobbered his pounding head.

Bad enough that last night had been long and agonizing as he'd stared up at his bedroom ceiling, angry at her for calling him out, but mostly angry at himself for his behavior. But then she'd shown up at his house...

And he'd wanted her anyway.

So much so, his frightening need had caused him to come completely unhinged, and now he felt damaged. Ripped open, bleeding and exposed, and he grappled with the rising lump of terror.

Because he'd wanted her, but she'd come here only because she still clung to the hope he was some sort of friggin' closet humanitarian. Well, he'd cleared that notion up. He'd snatched off those sunshiny-colored glasses of hers and stomped on them within an inch of their life. And then he'd run them over, just to be sure.

His gut slowly cinched tighter, hating that he'd had to say all those words.

And he suddenly realized he *wasn't* the same person he'd been last night. He had finally figured out why making love to Jessica was different.

Because he cared what she thought of him.

The terrifying realization dwarfed him, looming over his consciousness. He'd spent a lifetime earning a reputation for not giving a rat's ass about people's opinions of him, and now, he finally did.

Damn, he'd vowed to never put himself through that kind of agony again.

He closed his eyes, remembering the naive seven-year-old who used to wait by the phone for his dad to call. After his father had driven away and left him behind, Cutter had desperately clung to the hope it wasn't over. So he'd left messages on his father's voice mail. His dad's return calls grew fewer and farther between, until Cutter's ninth birthday. After that, there was only silence. On the day of his tenth birthday, Cutter called to leave yet another message, and got a number-no-longer-in-service recording.

And Cutter had finally given up the last bit of optimism he'd had left.

He frowned, swimming in a sea of suck. But then Jessica Wilson, the consummate Pollyanna, had shown up and dragged him down the path of hope again, only to crush the tender, spring-like growth.

Body tense, he lifted his lids, scanning Jessica's lovely face again. Worried he was squashing her, he shifted slightly.

Her eyes flew open. "Wait," she said, her fingers increasing their grip on his forearm.

He hesitated, hating the intense uncertainty in her face. But as long as he lived he would never forget her big, you-just-shot-me, Bambi eyes when he'd finally come clean about Cutter Thompson.

The Wildcard…asshole extraordinaire.

With a curse, Cutter rolled off, instantly missing the feel of Jessica's skin. The sweat cooled his body, leaving him chilled. He tugged on his swimsuit as he stared down at her. He could never be the kind of guy she wanted.

He couldn't even come *close*.

"Jessica, I'm the man you'd pass over in your online list of potential dates." He raked a hand through his hair and then dropped it to his side in defeat. "Every single time."

Jessica blinked. The expression on her beautiful face did nothing to deny his claim.

His heart pumped like the pistons of an engine doing a thousand rpms, because a man couldn't spend his whole life being left behind by those he cared about. He remembered too well how it wreaked havoc on the psyche.

Of course, the devastating events by the pool had already laid waste to his last protective barrier. Cutter had feared nothing on the track, least of all death, but the terror inside him now forced him to go on.

"I won't survive the cut being compared to the guy to my left and my right," he said. "In a list of my pros and cons, the cons win by a mile." Unable to stop himself, his pounding chest painful, he swept a sweat-soaked strand of hair from her forehead, his eyes holding hers. "I think we both know this has to end."

Not trusting himself to wait for a response, he turned and headed into his house, quietly shutting the door behind him.

CHAPTER ELEVEN

"AND she was constantly complaining about my dog." The middle-aged, balding man blew his nose into a handkerchief and looked around the circle of divorce survivors sitting in the reception area of Perfect Pairs, clearly looking for support. "She *never* liked Darth," he went on, sniffing with a mix of anger and allergies. "And when she told me it was either her or the mutt, I told her at least Darth Vader never mocked my love for Civilization."

Bewildered, Jessica stared at him. "Civilization?"

The man blinked at her, eyes watering, either from hay fever or emotional pain. "The computer game."

"Oh, yes," Jessica said. She didn't know whether to be amused, disgusted or disheartened by the man's reasons for ending his marriage. And when the perfect reply escaped her, she simply cleared her throat and glanced at her watch, grateful the hour of horror was finally over. "Well…" she said, forcing a smile for the circle of faces, "if no one else has anything to share, why don't we call it an evening?"

There was a chorus of murmuring voices as the small band of people gathered their belongings. Jessica rose from her seat on the couch. With a combination of dread and relief, she saw the last of the support-group attendees out the door, locking it behind them.

One obstacle cleared. Now she had the worst one to go.

A knot of anxiety gnawed at her insides, and she turned and leaned her back against the door, closing her eyes. Cutter had left a message about their final session, the one she'd been too distracted by the events at the pool to discuss. And, too chicken to call him on the phone, she'd texted him back. Thank God he'd agreed to meet her here tonight to post his last question for the contest. She couldn't stomach the thought of returning to his home.

Memories of the blow-up by the pool three days ago washed through her. His anger. Her crushing disappointment.

And the combustible desire.

A burn began in her belly, her palms grew damp and she longed for a chilled glass of wine. Because, after all the eventful emotions, Cutter's text had seemed so normal, including a little sarcastic comment that had made her laugh.

When he'd told her it was over, intellectually she'd had to agree, but her body—and a big chunk of her heart—had screamed *no*.

Jessica threaded her fingers through her hair, trying to soothe the war being waged inside. It had been an ongoing battle since she'd first fallen under Cutter's spell, and she should be grateful he'd done what she'd been too weak to do to date. Last night she'd walked the hallway in her home, searching for an answer to the Cutter conundrum.

But there wasn't one. And in her rather extensive history of setting herself up for failure—in marriage, in dating—this one would be legendary.

Worth its own wing in the Romance Blunders Hall of Fame.

Unfortunately, her relationship with Cutter was doing more than just messing with her head, it was also mucking up the rest of her well-ordered life. She never used to feel irritated during the support groups before, impatient with the occasional silly reasons for the end of a marriage. And she hadn't had time to continue her search for the right guy because she was too busy wanting to be with the *wrong* one.

And when had her parents realized they were wrong for each other?

The thought snuck up on her, and once it had made itself known, she couldn't ignore it. What had caused her parents to wake up one morning, look at each other, and think—hey, this isn't working out? Had they started out good together and slowly grown apart? Or were they just a bad match to begin with?

Like her and Cutter.

The sadness that had been building for years threatened to breech the dam and come pouring out. Her parents' divorce. Her own. Now Cutter. And though she'd always strived for optimism, it was growing harder and harder to maintain.

She rubbed her forehead, smoothing away the frown lines, turning the questions over in her head. But leaning here against this door wasn't going to solve her problems. And no one liked a whiner either. She had to somehow prepare for Cutter's arrival.

With a sigh, she straightened her shoulders and headed down the hallway towards her office. As she crossed the threshold, she spotted Cutter at her desk. She stopped short, but her heart kept going, slamming into the front of her chest.

He was thumbing through one of her brochures, one hip perched on the edge of her desk, muscular legs bared beneath his shorts. When he looked up at her, her world reduced itself to the masculine cut of his face and his expression—as if he was just as clueless how to handle her as she was him.

She held her breath for the umpteenth time since she'd met the man. Much more training like this and she'd be ready for an underwater-swimming competition. All the way across the blue waters of the Atlantic and back. Or maybe green... like Cutter's eyes.

It was a moment before he spoke. "Are Sneezy and his merry band of pessimists finally gone?"

Her legs finally remembered their purpose in life, and she moved to the chair opposite the desk, slowly lowering herself into the seat. "How long have you been here?"

"Long enough to hear that the computer-gaming geek should get rid of his dog or make an appointment for allergy shots."

"But how did you get in?"

His lips twisted dryly. "Through the front door. No one noticed me go by. You all were too engrossed in the story about the cheating ex."

She shook her head lightly, trying to focus on the conversation. How could he act so normal? "There were two cheating stories tonight."

"The one whose wife was supposed to be a computer analyst for the CIA." He tossed the brochure onto her desk and shot her a skeptical look. "Must be shocking to discover that, in lieu of the Pentagon, your spouse was working the street corner in front of the local crappy motel."

They stared at each other, and Cutter looked as if he was waiting for her to respond. But she'd exhausted her ability for status quo conversation with Cutter after their explosion by the pool. As the seconds passed without a comment from her, the atmosphere grew strained. Until Cutter leaned forward, his eyes intent on hers.

"Why do you do it?" he asked, his face radiating curiosity. Her nerves stretched tighter, and when she didn't answer, he went on. "The support group." He seemed genuinely interested, no mocking tone. "Why is someone who is so bound and determined to look on the bright side of life actively seeking out other people's misery?"

There wasn't much of a bright side to see lately. She dropped her gaze to the armrest of her chair, tracing the pattern in the wood with her finger, her mind turning the question over. "I find it helpful to hear why other people failed."

When he didn't reply, she looked up, and Cutter's expression was doubtful. "How does listening to the million and one ways people botch their relationships benefit you?"

With a small frown, she combed her fingers through the tips of her hair. "I think I know why *my* marriage ended. But my parents' is a complete mystery." Cutter was watching her, clearly expecting more of an explanation. She wished she had one for him.

"What excuse did they give?" he said.

"They said they didn't want to be married anymore."

"Sounds honest enough to me."

The old guest that had been rattling around the empty hallways of her heart stopped and faced her head-on. Refused to let her pass. Her brows drew together, and her whole face felt tight. "Well, that's not good enough." Embarrassed by the words, Jessica closed her eyes, rubbing her forehead, trying to ease the tension. "For the first fourteen years of my life they seemed perfectly happy." She dropped her hand to her lap and looked at Cutter. "And then one night at dinner they simply announced it was over."

His eyebrows slowly crept higher, and then he leaned back, hands on the edge of the desk, as if trying to process the news. "Just like that?" He hesitated, as if waiting for more. But there *wasn't* anymore, and that was the hardest part to fathom. It felt so incomplete. Cutter tipped his head and said, "You had no idea something was wrong?"

Her chest grew tight, and she dropped her attention to her skirt, smoothing out nonexistent wrinkles and trying to ignore the ache in her heart. "None whatsoever. They never fought in front of me. They seemed happy." Still focused on her lap, she linked her fingers together. "The week my father moved out of the house, I sat in my bedroom, waiting for them to tell me it was all a mistake—all the while they were calmly discussing how to divvy up the furniture." After sixteen years of marriage their conversation had been reduced to who would get what. Her voice dropped an octave, the memory washing over her. The disbelief. The grief. And the *confusion*. "And all I wanted to do was scream."

The silence that followed was loud, and when she looked up, Cutter was studying her with an expression that she couldn't decipher. Jessica had a powerful urge to fill in the gap with something.

Anything.

"Most people say I should be grateful the end was amicable." She gave a little laugh that sounded pathetic. "My parents told me the same thing."

Stunned, Cutter stared at her, until a small scowl overtook his face. "To hell with what they say, Jessica," he said softly. And when he went on, each word was enunciated clearly, emphasizing his point. "You do not have to feel grateful."

Her lids stung from the threat of tears and her lips twitched at one corner, a mix of a forlorn smile and a grimace. "Cutter Thompson says I'm allowed to feel like shit about it?"

His eyes held hers. There was no cynicism, no suppressed humor, just the frank gaze that never failed to draw her in. "Cutter Thompson says you are allowed to feel like shit about it."

She stared up at him, moved by the emotion in his voice. After all these years, it was odd to have someone give her permission to still feel sad.

And how could someone so wrong for her feel so *right*?

Because currently Cutter was looking at her as if he wanted to hold her. To comfort her. Every cell in her body leaned in his direction, wanting—needing—him to do just that. But it was the set of his posture that told the complete story.

Much as he might want to, he was not going to take her in his arms.

The ache that had started when he'd called it off grew

deeper, and the ripple of confusion grew wider. He was one of the most truthful people she'd ever encountered. He might avoid discussing his feelings, but he was always honest when he did. Often brutally so. He'd told her from that first day in the garage that he was all about Cutter Thompson. The more she'd grown to enjoy the bad boy's company, the more she'd needed to believe his claim wasn't true. But that wasn't his fault. It was hers.

More importantly, she'd heard the remorse in his words, seen the doubt in his face when he'd told her the truth by the pool. Cutter had come face to face with his mistakes and it had been clear he was questioning the choices he'd made. And didn't that constitute a positive change?

Cutter cleared his throat and sat back, and the moment was gone. "So what's the last Battle question going to be?"

She had several burning questions she'd like to ask.

Had they just been exploring their mutual appreciation of each other's bodies? Had they become friends with oh-so-not-boring benefits?

Or had they been—*could* they be—more?

Heart pounding, she finally settled on the new plan that had eluded her last night, and offered up the idea that was so close to her heart that it hurt.

"How about…" her voice faltered a fraction, but she pressed on. "What's a deal-breaker in a relationship?"

He lifted a brow dryly. "Doesn't sound particularly optimistic."

"Maybe it is," she said as she leaned forward, her heart rate climbing higher. "We're two intelligent adults. Maybe we haven't reached our own deal-breaker yet." His lids flickered in surprise, but she refused to chicken out, and hope was taking hold of her. Driving her forward. Because she couldn't stand the thought of the two of them being done.

She clamped her hand in a fist. "Maybe if we're willing to try—"

"Try?" he said, cutting her off. "Sunshine," he said, the flash of emotion crossing his face not encouraging, "I'll agree you're an intelligent woman." He folded his arms, giving her that boldly frank appraisal that often ended with him saying something she didn't want to hear. "But right now you're not being smart."

They were the same words that had been whispering in her head since their fight over Emmanuel. But that seemed like a lifetime ago.

His eyes perused her face, and her apprehension grew as he went on, his voice low. "And you know what else I think?"

Her fingers gripped the wooden armrests, troubled by his tone. She didn't respond to his question, afraid to hear his thoughts.

He went on anyway. "I think you're stuck on an endless manhunt because the guy you're looking for doesn't exist," he said, the words knocking her even further off kilter.

How could he say that? "That's not true. I'm just looking for…" The words sputtered, struggling to gain traction as her mind scrambled to get the statement right. "I'm just looking for…"

"The Prince of Darkness?" he said dryly.

"No."

The sarcasm disappeared. "A shinier shiny object?"

"No."

The look he shot her held no mercy. "Perfection?"

"No."

His eyes scanned hers, as if trying to read the answer in her face. "Then why do you keep rejecting every man that comes your way? They couldn't all have been crying about their ex-wives and living in their parents' garage."

She refused to let his cynical views belittle her priorities. And his words reminded her of exactly how far Cutter Thompson had to go. "I want someone who will work with me." She lifted an eyebrow that was aimed squarely at him.

"I don't want to get involved with another man who emotionally retreats and refuses to discuss where the relationship is going wrong."

The pause was longer than she expected, and when it ended, Cutter's expression had shifted from not encouraging to actively *dis*couraging.

"Is that how it was with Steve?" Cutter's eyes narrowed. "You telling him where he was going wrong?" His tone implied the conversation encompassed more than just her ex. It was personal.

"No," she said, hating that she was growing defensive. And hating even more that she felt the need to explain. "I just suggested he see a marriage counselor with me, or at least *consider* looking at a few books that might help," she said, gesturing to her bookshelf in the corner to her left.

Cutter faced the direction she was pointing, his whole body radiating his reservation as he gave the floor-to-ceiling shelves the once-over. "What are those?"

"Books on relationships."

The doubt and disbelief were huge. "*All* of them?"

His questioning tone held more than its fair share of accusation, and she bit back a retort as he rose from his seat to survey her collection.

As Jessica fought to control her irritation, Cutter pulled down a book and began to flip through the well-worn pages—his movements growing slower and slower, until the frown gradually overtook his entire face. He pulled down a second one entitled *How to Strengthen Your Marriage* and gave it a quick skim. The margin markings on this one were even more pronounced.

"Christ, Jessica," he said, raising his head to stare at her, his expression giving way to one of complete shock. "And I thought I was screwed up."

A cold hand gripped her heart. She'd expected sarcasm

from him, not a frustrating mix of censure and pity. "What are you talking about?"

"Your insecurities are incapacitating."

Anger sent her bolting from her seat, infuriated by his audacious claim. "Well I don't need a man whose first instinct when threatened by an idea is to *insult* me and push me away."

His green eyes, simultaneously brutally hard and painfully honest, bored into hers. "Yes, I was rude to Emmanuel, but I am not insulting you. I am telling you like it is. But you're so busy clinging to those damn everything's-just-fine glasses that you want to ignore the truths that are too inconvenient for you."

She planted a hand on her hip. "And which truth would *that* be?"

"Like the fact that you *drove* your husband away."

With a frigid flash, her heart froze, sending icy crystals through her veins, the shards stinging as they went and draining the blood from her face. "That is not true," she ground out. Her heart hammered at a pace that seemed to shake her whole body.

"Yes, it is." Cutter stepped closer. He wasn't angry. The only thing radiating from his face was absolute conviction. "Not only do you *not* want the guy to the left or the right, you don't want the guy right in front of you. You want to change him. Turn him into your ideal man. You haul out your books, tell him where he went wrong and give him a list to follow." Still clutching the hardcover, he held it up higher, more in frustration than anger. "Who could live with that?"

"I do not have lists."

Cutter barked out a scoff and turned the book in his hand, displaying a page. "What do you call this?"

She stared at the text she had marked up, passages underlined, notes scribbled in the margins…and fluorescent highlights through the author's bullet points on how to argue effectively.

The ice crystals vaporized from the flaming heat that swept up her face. "I just wanted Steve—"

"No," he said, slapping the book closed and cutting her off. "That's the problem. You didn't want Steve. You wanted the idealized version of him."

Her whole body rejected his claim, her mind circling in a whirlpool of disbelief, desperately scrabbling for the safety of logic. "There is nothing wrong with trying to improve yourself."

Cutter's face went so hard it could have deflected a bullet at close range. "Let me be the one to tell you how demoralizing living with that would be." He tossed the book to her desk, and it landed with a loud thump that echoed in her small office. "I spent my entire childhood *not* being wanted by my parents. And until I was ten years old, I thought if I tried a little harder, was a better kid, a little *nicer,* more *agreeable*—" the sarcasm dripped from his voice "—one of them might change their mind." The awful words hung between them, and Jessica's eyes began to burn. "But my dad left and never came back, and my mother never stopped talking about how her life got worse after I was born." He raked his fingers through his hair, spiking his bangs in all directions, and his tone morphed from hard cynicism to biting bitterness. "So put me down as someone who refuses to try and *improve* myself anymore."

Years of adulation from his adoring fans could never undo the damage done by those who really mattered—rejecting him time and again. The tragic reality of his past added to her pain, boosting her sorrow exponentially, and her chest grew tight again, making it impossible to breathe. Everything about Cutter, the anger, the cynicism, and even the no-holds-barred honesty suddenly became clear. Unfortunately, the knowledge came too late. "You know what the problem with your theory is?" she said quietly.

"No," he said, his voice dangerously low. "But I bet you're about to spell it out for me."

She ignored the dig and pushed on, before she collapsed from the feeling of futility. "You've given up." She shook her head, sadness overwhelming her. "No, that's not true. You haven't just stopped trying, you go out of your *way* to tick people off. But it hasn't made you happy."

The hot color of anger tinted his cheeks. "And you're so blinded by everyone else's faults that you can't see your own."

She blinked back the burning threat of tears, realizing that she hadn't fully grasped the extent of their relationship. They weren't just wrong for each other...

They were *bad* for each other.

And the misery ended all hope for any kind of a future with Cutter Thompson. "I think you can handle the last debate alone."

Eyes dark, he said, "I think you're right."

And with that, Cutter pivoted on his heel and left.

Cutter parked the 'Cuda at the curb in front of the Boys and Girls Club, wondering what the hell he was doing here. After calling Steve to locate Emmanuel's whereabouts, and then learning the news about the kid's latest troubles, coming had seemed the right thing to do. Now he wasn't so sure. Of course, nothing felt right anymore.

And he doubted it ever would again.

Gut churning, he gripped the gearshift, remembering how *alive* he'd felt the night he was here with Jessica. It had been six days since he'd last seen her. Six horrendous, crappy days that had felt like infinity.

After their blowup, he'd stormed home and finished the competition alone. Annoyed with every response his contestants had sent, he'd bitten his tongue—or his texting fingers, in this case—and finished the job. Numb from his fight with

Jessica, he'd suffered through two hours of response after response, forcing himself to participate.

With the competition over, and the benefit dinner behind him, he'd buried himself in his work, finishing the 'Cuda and focusing on his new business. He'd ordered the equipment for the shop, and had even hired a third mechanic to start next month. All in all, Cutter's life was back on track.

But with Jessica gone, it felt as if every bad event in his life—his dad, his mom and his horrific career-ending wreck—had all been rolled into one and magnified by a hundred.

A fresh wave of agony bowled over him, and he dropped his head back against the seat and closed his eyes. Since he'd left Jessica's office, his mind had been spinning its wheels but never gaining traction. He'd been stuck in a never-ending neutral hell. Time and again he'd contemplated seeking her out, and to heck with how sorry he'd be in the end. Or how much it would cost his dignity to be with someone who didn't *really* want him, outside of the sexual sense of the word.

He would have shoved aside every semblance of self-respect and groveled like that seven-year-old boy who'd chased his father down the road. Or the ten-year-old who had sat by the phone, waiting for his dad to call him back.

But he couldn't get past the memory of Jessica's expression when he'd accused her of causing the destruction of her marriage. In honor of the cocky bastard he used to be, and apparently *still* could be, he'd dragged out her painful past and flogged it again, ensuring the wounds would be fresh forever.

These last six days, it was the image of her devastated expression by the bookshelf—juxtaposed with the you-just-shot-me, Bambi eyes by the pool—that had precipitated his perpetual orbit around the ninth circle of hell.

And while he'd finally concluded he could never fix things between the two of them, he could at least mend one fence he'd smashed. And maybe it would make up for a little of the pain he'd inflicted on Jessica, as if, in some minor way, he could become the man she'd hoped she'd seen in him all along.

He blew out a breath and stared at the Boys and Girls Club. Steve had said Emmanuel would probably be here. But if Cutter sat here any longer, the boy would leave and the opportunity would be gone.

With renewed determination, Cutter exited the 'Cuda and entered the building. When he asked about the kid, the grayhaired lady at the front desk directed him out back, and Cutter passed through the beautiful new gym where a dozen teens were playing basketball.

He eventually found Emmanuel outside, alone, shooting hoops on an old concrete court. Unlike the teens inside who wore athletic wear, Emmanuel was dressed in black cargo pants and a black T-shirt that swallowed his tall, lanky body. His hair was dyed an unnatural color that matched his clothes.

When the teen caught sight of Cutter, his face reflected the mood of his dark attire. "Why are you here?"

"To talk to you." Cutter waited a moment, feeling totally out of his element. Being on the receiving end of an adoring teen had been easy in comparison to the stone wall he now faced; Emmanuel had obviously changed his mind about the Wildcard.

Smart kid.

Cutter went on. "Heard you were caught racing a few days ago and got tossed in the clinker overnight."

"What's it to you? You're not my dad, so beat it."

Cutter regarded him for a moment. The animosity seeping from the kid was daunting. But, instead of leaving, Cutter crossed to a box of basketballs, pulled one out and sat on the ball. He stared at the teen, the wall of fury seemingly unscalable. "Don't have a clue how to go fatherly on a teen." He gave a small shrug. "My old man split when I was a kid."

Emmanuel cast him a scathing look. "Yeah?" He took the jump shot, missing by a mile. "So cry me a river."

Cutter's forehead wrinkled in brief amusement. It was interesting to be on the receiving end of his teenage self. "I also heard you got fired at the auto parts store as a result of your escapade."

This time Emmanuel didn't even acknowledge his presence, dribbling down the court and successfully planting a hook shot. When the ball bounced to the ground, the teen begin making shots from the foul line, his back facing Cutter.

Damn, disagreeable was hard to hold a conversation with.

But Cutter tried again. "I'm here to offer you a job."

"I don't want your charity."

"Gonna be hard to get hired anywhere with a record."

"So?" Like a cannon, Emmanuel shot the ball and it slapped against the backboard, the sound echoing on the small court.

A part of Cutter wanted to give up. He didn't need this. He had a fledgling business to get back to. Taking on an angry teen would hardly be the smart thing to do.

He swiped a hand through his hair and stared at the boy's back, remembering all the times Jessica had hunted him down. No matter how rude he'd been, or undeserving of her efforts, she still had come back.

At least until he'd accused her of destroying her marriage and killed all hope of her retaining any lingering affection.

The knifing pain in his chest didn't come from his now-healed rib injury. It was from the band encircling his heart, making each breath hurt. But he'd spent a lifetime feeling sorry for himself and he was tired of the emotion.

And it was time to just step up and take the higher road. At least put in the effort to *be* the better person, instead of going out of his way to piss everyone off.

Just like Emmanuel.

Cutter stood, picked up his ball and found a new location

on the sidelines, balancing on his makeshift seat. From this angle, he could see the profile of the teen's face, but the boy continued to mutely dribble his ball, clearly unhappy with Cutter's persistent presence.

With a sigh, Cutter said, "It's easy to blame yourself when a parent splits."

Emmanuel's hand fumbled briefly on the ball, but he recovered quickly. But the scowl that had settled on his face was *Psycho,* knife-through-the-shower-curtain worthy.

Cutter had definitely scored a hit with his comment.

"'Course, I was pretty little when my dad took off," Cutter said, feeling stupid, but staying anyway. "But for a long time I thought if I'd been a better kid, he wouldn't have left…"

His voice died as he remembered all those times his dad had dropped him off after a visit. Cutter would sit on the front porch, wondering why the man always left. After his father had moved, Cutter had manned the chair next to the phone, dreaming of the day his father would come back for good. Hoping his old man would come clean about why he'd left, and maybe even convince his mother it wasn't because of Cutter.

He blinked, pushing the memory aside. Dumb dreams. They'd never done him any good. But Jessica was right.

Adopting the screw-the-world attitude hadn't helped either.

Elbows on his knees, fingers linked, Cutter watched Emmanuel ignore him and said, "Take it from someone who's been there. The anger will eat you up if you let it." The kid continued to bounce the ball, and Cutter wasn't sure if the surly teen was listening or not. If he was anything like Cutter at that age, probably not. "I let it control me when I bumped Chester, and I blew my racing career." Funny how that didn't hurt near as much as losing Jessica. His breath escaped with a whoosh, and he swiped a frustrated hand through his hair. "Not the kind of thing a hero does."

The pause was filled with the sound of a dribbling ball as Emmanuel continued to refuse to acknowledge his presence. After several minutes passed with no response from the kid, Cutter pushed up to his feet. He'd said his piece. He'd made his offer.

It was up to the kid either to accept it or not.

"I'll leave my number inside in case you change your mind," Cutter said.

CHAPTER TWELVE

TRYING to work, Jessica sat in her office, used tissues strewn across her desk, eyes puffy from lack of sleep. The frequent crying binges weren't helping their appearance either.

It had been exactly seven days since Cutter had walked out, and she'd spent most of it bawling her eyes out. A massive crying jag that had been thirteen years in the making. And once she had started, she couldn't seem to stop.

She'd indulged in a whine festival that would put most vineyards to shame.

Some of her tears were a little girl's grief over the end of what she had *thought* was a happy family, and some were a grown woman's hurt over Cutter's claim she had ruined her marriage.

But the biggest trigger by far was the unbearable pain of missing Cutter.

An ache the size of the Atlantic had taken up residence in her heart, and there was no ignoring this unwanted guest. Every time she closed her eyes, the horrid memory of Cutter's past, and his stunned expression at the bookshelf—one part censure and two parts pity—had hit her again. And yet, despite everything he'd said to her, she missed his cutting sarcasm, his cynical take on life, and that rare almost-smile that lit her world.

Toss in her body's intense longing for the fire in his touch, and she was a mess of gigantic proportions.

Between the huge hole Cutter had left in his wake and the nagging fear that she might have messed up worse than the majority of the ludicrous divorce stories she'd heard over the years, she wasn't getting much rest.

She was hoping her personal, in-depth exploration into the effects of sleep deprivation would end soon—but so far, no such luck. Especially on the night Cutter was supposedly sitting at the charity banquet with Calamity Jane.

By all accounts the dinner had been a huge hit. The Brice Foundation had made more money than ever before. And what had started as a potential publicity disaster had ended on a personal one of cataclysmic proportions.

For the millionth time since Cutter's awful claim, her gaze drifted to the wall sporting the shelves of self-help books. At first she'd been too angry for an objective look, convinced that Cutter had lashed out in his usual fashion, choosing to come out swinging when he felt pushed into a corner. But as time had passed, she remembered the open honesty in his eyes, the conviction in his voice, and—most damning by far—the lack of anger. Doubt had taken hold, and the shelf had loomed larger and larger, until now it was an ominous beast that seemed to sop up every oxygen molecule from the room.

It was draining her of any capacity for hope, much less optimism.

Miserable, Jessica slumped deeper into her chair, eyeing the tower of books warily. To be so thoroughly paralyzed by a stack of paper and ink was dispiriting. To be forced to live without Cutter was brutal.

Heart thumping painfully, her mind pushed away the implications of the thought. Her precarious—and entirely questionable—ability to function could shut down altogether if she began to explore why she missed Cutter.

Fear squeezed her chest at the idea. "God," she said, and snatched up her cell phone. Facing her past had to be easier than facing her feelings for Cutter. She dialed Steve's number, and when he answered, she didn't bother with a hello. "When did you first realize it wasn't going to work?"

She heard jazz music in the background. "Jess?" he said, his voice confused. "You haven't returned my calls. I've been worried—"

"I'm talking about us, Steve," she said. She took a breath and forced herself to slow down. It had been five years since their divorce. Giving him a minute to catch up would only be fair. "I want to know when you first thought we were a mistake."

"Jess," Steve groaned. There was no confusion now, only a man who didn't want to have this conversation. And she was very familiar with the reluctant tone. "It hardly matters any—"

"Don't," she said. More evasion on Steve's part. Or maybe it was simply a delay tactic. She remembered those, too. The jazz music in the background took on a lively tune, and her fingers clamped harder around her phone. "When was the first time you remember thinking you wanted out?" When the moment stretched to uncomfortable levels, Jessica said, "The truth, Steve." She hoped she wasn't hurting her cellular with her grip. "Please."

The sound of his sigh was loud. "I guess it would be when the CEO of the Wallace Corporation was flying down from New York for our meeting."

Stunned, Jessica sat up in her chair. The visit had taken place only four months into a marriage that had lasted for fifteen. Shock made her words sluggish. "You were positive he was going to hate your presentation."

Steve had never been a workaholic before, and his late hours and distracted mindset had started to wear her down.

She knew he'd been working hard, but a little part of her had been hurt.

And worried.

Okay, actually she'd been scared stiff. Especially after she flipped through a woman's magazine and landed on a survey that asked the readers how they first realized their relationship was in bad straits. The working-late excuse had been the number-one-reported sign.

Looking back, the fear seemed terribly ridiculous, but it had felt so *real*.

"Yes," Steve went on. "The morning of the presentation I was stressed and forgot to say goodbye when I left. After I got home, you asked if I was mad at you. But when I said no…you didn't believe me." His pause was longer this time, but there was a ton of meaning in the silence. Her heart grew heavy, and he went on. "It took me two hours to persuade you it wasn't a sign of a bigger issue."

She didn't bother to tell him that, deep down, she'd never really believed it wasn't. Four months later, after multiple similar episodes, and with Steve burying himself further in his work, she'd purchased her first book. She remembered the look on Steve's face when she brought it home. But that was nothing compared to his horrified expression when she purchased the second one three weeks later. At the time, she thought he was avoiding talking about their problems.

And it had certainly never occurred to her that *she* might be the biggest part of the problem.

Defeated, she slumped back in her chair. "Why didn't you tell me?" she said.

"I tried." Steve's sigh was huge. "But you weren't picking up on my hints."

Hints. She scrunched up her face, trying to recall any clues. But if he'd been tossing them out, she had missed every one. "Why didn't you just flat out *tell* me?"

Steve's voice went low. "Come on, Jess," he said softly.

Clearly he hadn't felt the direct route was an option. "You wouldn't have believed me. And all I would have accomplished was to hurt your feelings."

Jessica closed her eyes.

It's not you, it's me.

It's not your crippling insecure ways—it's my reluctance to tell you that you're driving me insane.

She stared blankly at the wall beyond her desk, the truth settling around her like an ugly, uncomfortable dress. She could have spent the rest of her life lining up the world's most perfect male, but it still wouldn't have worked. Because she'd always insisted on picking the *nice* guys—when all along what she'd needed was a brash, ex-race-car driver with a cutting mouth, a whole lot of attitude...

And a penchant for brutal honesty.

She needed Cutter Thompson because she was in love with him, and no one else would ever be more right.

Jessica blinked against the instant sting beneath her lids, knowing it was now an artesian well of tears that would never stop. Her nose grew stuffy, and she sniffed, reaching for another tissue in her severely dwindling supply.

"What's up with you and Cutter?" Steve said quietly, clearly oblivious to the momentous revelation she'd just endured, and that the answer to his question was so complicated it required its own internet support forum. There was concern in Steve's voice. "Do I need to send someone over to break his knees?"

"No." Jessica planted her elbow on her desk, wearily resting her forehead on her palm. "I'm the one who messed up."

The silence was long and heavy as Jessica waited for Steve to ask what else was new. Instead, he said, "So what's your plan?"

Jessica looked at the wall of books that had been read, reread, highlighted and underscored within an inch of their printed little lives. There was nothing on those shelves that could help her with Cutter. There was no analyzing her way out of the mess she'd created, and logic wouldn't solve her problems.

Ultimately, the only thing strong enough to overcome it all was her love for Cutter.

"No plan," she said, her heart tapping harder. "I'll just have to improvise."

Jessica followed her GPS to the upscale industrial park located in a high-end business district. It wasn't hard to identify which building was Cutter's. The 'Cuda parked in front was a dead giveaway.

It was strange to see the car in the parking lot lined with oak trees. Glossy black, the new coat of paint glistened in the sun. The brawny vehicle oozed raw power, as if poised to release its barely restrained speed at a moment's notice. Just the right touch, and all the pent-up energy would be unleashed. Much like its owner.

Memory welled higher, and Jessica's body went taut as she parked next to the 'Cuda. With a growing apprehension, she eyed the front of the building. The gargantuan garage door to the left was closed, the sound of muted music thumping from within. Not The Boss, but someone she didn't recognize. Harder. Angrier.

Which didn't bode well for Cutter's mood.

Her stomach slid lower in her belly, and she shifted her gaze to the smaller office door on the right, gnawing on her lip, gathering her courage. Improvising didn't seem like a good idea now that she was confronted with actually pulling it off. But loving Cutter and living without him was torment. Her heart lurched every time she thought of him. And that was so frequent it was like a streaming banner in her mind—similar to the news feeds that ran along the bottom of the CNN channel.

When the office door opened and Cutter appeared in the

doorway, the scrolling news feed in her mind went ultra-caps, a deafening screaming in her brain. Jessica could barely muddle through the process of breathing. Battered jeans clung to his body, and a smudged T-shirt stretched across his chest. Cutter looked beautiful.

But gawking like an idiot wasn't going to get her any closer to ending her agony. Heart pounding, she exited her car and closed the door, hand clinging to the handle, eyes on Cutter. He was leaning against the open doorway, thumbs hooked in his belt loops, his face guarded. And she instantly knew this wasn't going to be easy. *Nothing* with Cutter had been easy. But there was more than just wariness in his expression.

Was he trying to decide how to tell her to leave?

Fear joined the mix of emotions, and she didn't step closer. Without any idea of where to start, she said, "How was the benefit dinner with your online groupie?"

The only movement on his face was the lift of a single brow. *"Groupies,"* he corrected, and it took a moment to sink in. Jessica frowned in confusion until Cutter went on. "Calamity Jane was four retired bridge-club ladies ranging from seventy-eight to eighty-two years old."

She did her best not to gape at him, floored by the news, trying to picture their dinner.

"It was a hell of a date," he added dryly.

A ghost of a smile flickered across Cutter's face, but his fatalistic undertones brought a familiar wave of sorrow. She longed to throw herself on the ground and tell him she was sorry for letting her doubts rule her actions. She wanted to rewind the clock and—after shooting a chastising email to her silly, insecure self—try again. To quit *pushing* so hard.

A breeze blew, rustling the oak overhead. Light played across Cutter's face, and Jessica's eyes wandered over the tall form of this man she loved.

The lean muscle, dark energy and raw edges.

But he was definitely looking at her as if there was something he wanted to say that she wouldn't like, and a tight knot of panic formed. The pressure beneath her artesian well of tears increased, and she briefly pressed her eyelids together, forcing them back. Because honest dialogue had to begin with, well—honest *dialogue.*

"I spoke to Steve today," she said. Cutter didn't say anything, just regarded her with that coiled-spring edginess, until shame pushed her on. "You were right. I drove him away."

Cutter's eyebrows moved a fraction higher and, as if sensing she was about to shovel out a pile of misgivings, odoriferous stench and all, he crossed the pavement to lean his back against the door of the 'Cuda. Now four feet from her, he folded his beautiful arms across his chest.

And waited.

She cleared her throat, pushing past the fear. "I was always overly aware of the little things," she said. "Worried they were signs of a pending relationship apocalypse."

Cutter's face gave nothing away, and she longed for some sort of emotion, even anger. At least then she'd know he felt *something.* But…nothing was forthcoming.

His words were careful. "Understandable, given the way your parents split."

Which was so much more leeway than she'd ever afforded him, and his childhood had been light years ahead of hers in the misery department. Her piddly complaints were insignificant in comparison.

Guilt hit, and she lifted a shoulder listlessly. "I guess so," she said. "It's just…" She smoothed the knotted muscles on her neck, trying to ease the tension. To explain her desperate, foolish behavior. "All these years I believed my marriage failed because I chose the wrong guy." She gave a laugh that was more humiliation than humor and dropped her hand. "It's hard to face the mistakes I've made."

His gaze held hers, as honest as ever. "I'm sure your heart was in the right place."

A tidal wave of remorse threatened to swamp her. He was generously giving her the benefit of the doubt, and she didn't deserve it. She didn't deserve *him*. Not once when confronted with his questionable behavior had she ever afforded him the same latitude.

Instead, she'd been critical. Every moment he'd failed to live up to her expectations, she'd made it clear.

It was time to come clean. "My list was nonsense," she said. When his expression didn't budge, the tiny bud of terror expanded in her chest, and her grip on the car-door handle grew tight. "For fourteen years I was absolutely sure my parents loved each other. And then suddenly, they didn't. And I've never trusted myself to recognize love—or the lack of—since." It was a pathetic excuse, and she knew it. She fisted her free hand at her side. All the worry and second-guessing that had paralyzed her for years piled higher, making the words difficult. "So I pressed Steve too hard and drove him away." She'd made a plan, set an expectation and pushed. Just like she'd pushed Cutter. Blinking back the sting of tears, she went on. "I just needed—"

"A guarantee it would work out?"

"Yes."

Cutter stared at her warily. "Hence the rules and lists."

Heat seared her face. "They were my pitiful way of trying to ensure I found the right guy." But nothing on her bookshelf applied to the man who challenged her views on life, shooting holes in her theories, one biting remark after another. "And you were so different from what I thought I needed to make a relationship succeed, it scared me." Her throat ached from the pressure of tears, and her words came out weak. "But I wanted you so much…"

Something flashed in his eyes. An emotion she didn't recognize. Whatever it was, it didn't look encouraging.

Pushing forward grew more difficult. "So I kept trying to turn you into something I'd recognize." She rubbed her temple wearily and sent him a frown that held all the helplessness she'd felt to date. "But you weren't following the rules."

"I rarely do."

"Which was disastrous for my comfort levels."

His pause was brief. "Which would continue if we stayed together."

Was he still writing the two of them off?

Anxiety spiraled in her belly, drawing it tight. "But, Cutter," she finally let go of the car and stepped closer, halving the distance between them, "you are *The One*." She looked up at him, pushing aside every crippling ocean of fear, hoping the truth showed on her face because she felt it to the deepest depths of her being. "We are perfect together. You are perfect for *me*." She mustered up a wobbly smile. "Many shades of gray and all." When he didn't respond, didn't even look *moved*, she played her final card. Her pièce de résistance. Jessica drew in a shaky breath and spoke the most honest words of her twenty-seven years. "Cutter, I'm in love with you."

His stupefied expression did nothing to alleviate her adrenaline-induced state. Every muscle in her body tensed, and she slowed her breaths to help control the ungodly rate of her heart. Overhead, trees shifted in the breeze. Leaves rustled. And the world waited for Cutter's reaction. She wasn't sure how long the pause lasted, but it felt as if she lived, died and was resurrected a hundred times over.

Until a squeaking sound split the air as the garage door was rolled up by someone inside, and a male voice called out, "Mr. Thompson?"

Heart still throbbing, dying for Cutter's reply to her confession, Jessica turned to find Emmanuel standing in the doorway to the garage.

The teen's gaze shifted warily between Jessica and Cutter. "I'm ready to tighten the calipers on the brakes."

It took several seconds for Cutter to respond. "Use the torque wrench."

Emmanuel looked at him skeptically, a hint of defiance in his tone. "What happens if I don't?"

Cutter nodded at the two-foot wrench the teen was holding. "That monstrosity you have in your hand might break the bolt."

Instantly the defiance in the boy's face was gone. "Oh," Emmanuel said. And with that, the dark-haired teen turned and headed back into the shop.

Stunned by the exchange and the implications behind the teenager's presence, Jessica was still trying to recover from the boy's appearance when she aimed her gaze at Cutter. "How long has he been here?"

"Two hours."

"How long has he been working on the brakes?"

"Two hours."

Something in his tone alerted her to his frustration. "How long would it have taken you?"

"Thirty minutes."

Jessica glanced at Emmanuel, watching him wrestle clumsily with his tool at the wheelbase of Cutter's sports car in the garage, and then turned her attention back to Cutter. Her mind was frantically trying to keep up with the unexpected event. "So where is the angle for Cutter Thompson?"

He paused, staring at her. "There isn't one."

Her gaze roamed his handsome face, the sea-green eyes, and the glints of gold in his brown hair. He'd faced so much and come so far, and she hadn't made it easy for him.

"Why?" she asked softly.

A moment passed as he returned her stare, as if struggling with his answer. "I guess I'm going for a paler gray." But before hope could take root inside her, reservation infiltrated his face. "But I'll never be a light enough shade for you."

The tears welled higher, burning her lids. "I've done nice

and it didn't work." She'd spent their entire relationship telling Cutter how he wasn't measuring up. No wonder he was looking at her with such monstrous misgivings. "I *need* the bad boy. You are the right guy, just as you are." She gave a watery sniff and tried to smile, but her mouth twitched with guilt. "And I promise to quit nagging."

His brow crinkled in instant irony. "Sunshine, nobody makes an ass-kicking more fun than you." His tone went dry. "Something I clearly need on a regular basis. But Jessica..." The reservation returned, and he plowed a hand through his hair.

The frustration in his gesture and the flash of hesitation in his eyes gave her the courage to step closer. She wasn't sure if his doubts were about the two of them or about his continued resistance to her pleas. Praying it was the latter, she placed a hand on his chest. His thumping heart beneath her palm matched hers. Her first solid clue to his emotion.

She stared up into all that uncertainty in his face. "Tell me what you're feeling."

Eyes troubled, he blew out a breath, until his expression eased a bit, the candid words full of self-derision. "All I know is, since I left you, I've been to hell and haven't been able to find my way back." The honesty in his face was encouraging, but the continual apprehension in his eyes was heartbreaking. His words came out low. "But I don't want to turn out like my parents."

This was about more than just their relationship. It was his past, and hers.

"What *do* you want?" she said.

With a small frown he brushed her hair from her forehead. When his answer came, it was simple, but it was all she needed to hear.

"You," he said. "I just want you."

Eyes burning with unshed tears, she clutched his shirt. "I *am* yours." When his apprehension didn't ease, she went on, her fingers crushing the cotton. "Cutter, I had the marriage license and failed. The legal route didn't work for our parents either. And all I really want—" She pressed her lips together, intent on getting it right. "The only part of the marriage vow I need from you is a promise of till death do us part."

Eyes pained, expression stark, he said, "Jessica, I love you so much it hurts to live without you." He looked at her with that love—and a measure of surrender—in his eyes. "Forever is the only way to end my misery."

The relief was profound. She leaned against him, and he wrapped his arms around her. With his heart beating beneath her ear, slowly she allowed herself to feel the joy, to let herself believe it was real. That somehow, somewhere during her Battle of the Sexes with the Wildcard, he'd fallen in love with her as well. It was almost too good to be true.

But she would never doubt the two of them.

Smiling, she looked up at him, relishing the hard muscle. The wall of steel. He stroked the small of her back, sending decadent messages to her body. Cutter's eyes grew dark, and her smile grew bigger as he leaned in for a kiss.

"Mr. Thompson?" Emmanuel called from inside the shop, and Cutter froze, lips halfway to hers. The teen's voice was triumphant. "I'm finished."

Cutter briefly closed his eyes. "Great timing," he muttered, his expression one of barely maintained patience, lips hovering above her mouth. "Would it be rude if I tossed him out so I could make love to you?" The long-suffering expression on his face was adorable.

"Extremely rude."

"Damn." He pursed his lips, as if considering his options. "And taking off in the 'Cuda for a repeat backseat rendezvous? Rude?" Gaze smoldering, he pulled her flush against him. "Or acceptably wicked?"

In response to his hard body, delight spread through her. "Definitely acceptable."

A brow lifted suggestively. "You in?"

"Absolutely," she said with a grin. "You see, I've developed a thing for the wicked boy with a bad attitude."

* * * * *

A sneaky peek at next month...

MODERN™

INTERNATIONAL AFFAIRS, SEDUCTION & PASSION GUARANTEED

My wish list for next month's titles...

In stores from 16th December 2011:

❑ The Man Who Risked It All – Michelle Reid

❑ The End of her Innocence – Sara Craven

❑ Secrets of Castillo del Arco – Trish Morey

❑ Untouched by His Diamonds – Lucy Ellis

In stores from 6th January 2012:

❑ The Sheikh's Undoing – Sharon Kendrick

❑ The Talk of Hollywood – Carole Mortimer

❑ Hajar's Hidden Legacy – Maisey Yates

❑ The Secret Sinclair – Cathy Williams

❑ Say It with Diamonds – Lucy King

Available at WHSmith, Tesco, Asda, Eason, Amazon and Apple